The Blade and the Passion

The Blade
and the Passion

*A Sprawling
Historical Romance*

Les Dawson

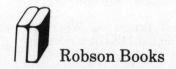

Robson Books

This Robson paperback edition first published in 1994
First published in Great Britain in 1993 by Robson Books
Ltd, Bolsover House, 5-6 Clipstone Street, London W1P 7EB

British Library Cataloguing in Publication Data
A catalogue record for this title is available from the
British Library

ISBN 0 86051 872 8 (hbk)
ISBN 0 86051 951 1 (pbk)

Printed in Great Britain by WBC Print and WBC
Bookbinders, Bridgend, Mid-Glamorgan

CONTENTS

AUTHOR'S PREAMBLE

No doubt, some clever dick with a double mortgage, a time-share in Cyprus and a car-phone will pick up this stirring chronicle and tell his friends that it's a load of rubbish. Everybody is, of course, entitled to his or her opinion, and if it is rubbish, well, at least it's British rubbish. I freely admit that the reader will discover some historical inaccuracies here and there, and I've got one or two dates mixed up too. I couldn't help it, I got fed up.

It's not easy, you know, sitting here, a typewriter and a bottle of Scotch my only companions. And life would be intolerable if I was to be denied a nip while I wrote. I'm not a hard drinker ... I find it very easy ... Ha, ha. Just have a small slug, excuse me for a moment ... That's better. This epic will, I trust, have your very senses reeling with its taut, intellectual style of factual prose ... Hang on, I'll just have another slurp ...

Now where was I? Oh yes, prose. History's all right, but let's face it, should we believe all we've been taught? S'funny, this bottle's half-empty already ... Stuff it, hey? ... Ooh, bloody 'ell, that's gone down well, hey? I said, hey? Got wind now ... better out than in, hey? Ha, ha, ha ... If you don't like the sodding book, up yours, mate. Heard a crackin' joke the other day ... What the hell was it? Bottle's nearly empty ... Bastards ...

Forgotten the bloody joke, hey, pal? . . . HEY, PAL?
WHY SHUD I HALF KILL MYSELF, RITING BUCKS
FOR YOU LOT? . . . GOING TO BE SICK IN A
MINUTE . . . JUST LET THE WIFE SAY ONE
THING . . . WISH ME MOTHER WAS HERE,
NOBODY CARES . . . I'M PISSED.

READERS' JOKE COMPETITION

Why did the pervert cross the road? . . . He thought the chicken was having an affair on Thursday!

(Anyone who's gone bald in a Tunisian bidet will appreciate the subtle undertones of this inspired offering from Miss Cattermole of Luton. Once engaged to a lighthouse architect in Bulgaria, she was for many a year a fine ventriloquist with a West African banjo orchestra who did a lot on army buses for geese with loose feet. Miss Cattermole now lives up a big hill in a rope warehouse, and likes to hold iced walnuts up her dress whilst the fire goes out. Miss Cattermole admits being over fifty, but looks a lot smaller.)

NOW READ ON . . .

THE TESTIMONY OF PIERRE LE TOQ: I

I confess that I had tired of Paris that burning summer. Most Parisians had fled to the coast or the mountains, and only the ragged dregs of humanity crept along the city boulevards under the merciless sun. There was a strong smell of horse-shit in the streets and, since the nightsoil men had gone on strike, the stench wafted through the open windows of the hunched houses on Rue Gor-Blimee.

I had hoped that, as a captain in the King's Musketeers, I could have accompanied the Monarch to his château above Grasse, but no. Instead, I had been ordered to stay in the capital, and continue the search for the phantom swordsman who opposed the King and held all France in the grip of fear. His name? It is one that will be scrawled in the book of the damned for all eternity . . . the 'Blade of Passion' . . . a romantic name for a pitiless rogue.

His deeds were whispered in the wine shops and brothels along the Seine . . . of how he had gelded a pork butcher in a whist-drive, after seeing the lustful tradesman grope a slender pot-boy behind a sack of yeast in a brewery; of the time he had speared a gypsy's anus from a distance of fifty yards with a wooden pike. Sluts, if they were to be believed, told of his love-making that was akin to a furnace of desire, of his mighty organ that drove women wild, and some to an all-night chemist.

Yet there seemed to be no real description of this fiend from hell. The only person who claimed to have met him, and lived to tell his cronies about it, was the bell-ringer of Notre-Dame, Quasimodo, and he was bent. Anyone can be ugly, I grant you, but Quasimodo abused the privilege. It wasn't just his hump or his lumpy lips; it wasn't even his ridiculous eyeballs, set about four feet apart. No, it was his tights that bugged me. They were pink with a leather gusset. Was he a poof? I think not. Unless you were a blind pervert from a Rheims monastery, you couldn't fancy Quasimodo. The twisted bell-ringer described the Blade of Passion as a short man on the tall side with a bald head and big ears; like a wing nut off a cart. When the phantom spoke, his accent suggested Normandy or perhaps Wolverhampton, and he had a habit of wiping his nose on his socks, which in turn indicated a flair for acrobatics or one hell of a big nose.

However, the rascal continued to elude capture, and I, for one, had grown weary of seeking him out. I longed for the arms of Madam du Barry, my mistress and private accountant. Oh, how I yearned for her heated flesh! My loins churned at the thought of her tattooed breasts thrusting out to me while she played the trombone. For the love of du Barry, I had killed a man in a pistol duel . . . he'd arrived with a sword and I had a pistol. For her favours, I had climbed Mont Blanc and chipped ice off the peak for her pink gin . . . I would have died for her. Her beauty intoxicated me beyond reason, and she'd given me a few winners at Longchamps. But she had gone with the King to the South of France, and I knew with a heavy heart that as I walked the city streets, she'd be having more piggy than pork luncheon meat.

My horse stopped outside the Place Pigalle and broke short my ponderings. As my sturdy steed evacuated its bowels on to the shit-encrusted cobbles, a massive, dark, bold woman bared her white teeth at me, then disappeared through a paint-blistered doorway. I dismounted and, with one hand on my sword hilt, followed the wanton. The only sounds to stir the sticky afternoon heat were the clank of my spurs, my horse farting and the cries of 'Encore' from a nearby public hanging.

Inside the hovel, the ugly frump waited, her breasts heaving up and down like billowing sails on a man o' war. She was certainly a big tart . . . the last time I'd seen dugs that big had been on a team of pregnant oxen.

'What is brown and sounds like a bell?' she whispered. I shook my head. She peered at me and spat. 'The answer to that riddle is dung.' With that, she pulled a bayonet from her drawers and lunged at me. I backed away, fell over a couple having it off on a hammock and the bayonet point pricked my throat.

Just then, a voice rang out. 'Stop! I wish to speak to him before he dies.'

The fat slut shoved the bayonet back into her knickers, and I rose gingerly to my feet. The couple beneath me asked if I fancied a glass of sherry and a threesome later on, so I snarled a hasty 'Yes' and gave them the address of a boarding house that provided sandwiches and a flute quartet during foreplay.

All of a sudden I saw the man who had saved my gizzard from ventilation, and I gasped. It was the Man in the Iron Mask! (I could tell that because he was wearing an iron mask.)

'You are a captain in my brother's Musketeers, are you not?' he said sharply.

I shook my head and replied stiffly, 'No, my name is Pierre Le Toq, not "Not".'

'Don't be such a bloody fool,' he muttered, banging his metal head against the wall. 'I have ways and means of making you Toq.' With that, he removed his iron mask and took a set of pinewood dentures from his mouth. He dropped them in a ewer of water, swished them around for a while, then popped them back in. 'I am the rightful heir to the throne,' he thundered. 'My brother had me abducted, then forced me to wear this iron mask for the rest of my life. Luckily my friend the Count of Monte Cristo helped me to escape, and Florence here –' he jabbed an Indonesian phallic symbol in the direction of the harlot with the bayonet – 'gave me shelter and a can of rust remover. She mistook you for one of my secret agents. Then, when you failed to answer the password, she assumed you were one of my brother's men.'

'But, sir, we thought you were still in the Bastille? Won't the King, I mean, your brother realize that you have escaped?' I asked this in an anxious tone, and my sincerity was noted. He patted me gently on the shoulder.

'Fear not, my dear Le Toq. My mother took my place in the Bastille. She likes it there. Every Thursday they play bingo and her iron mask's air-conditioned.'

That night I pledged allegiance to restoring the King's brother to the throne, and Florence felt my arse. In the space of a few hours I had made myself an outlaw, nay, a traitor, and now the future loomed before me, tinged with peril.

It was the Man in the Iron Mask's wish that I try to carry on as before, which was difficult, because Florence had removed my army issue pantaloons and was measuring my codpiece. She was so awful to look at, I wore blinkers.

Just then, a pock-marked ruffian entered the room and fell on his knees before the Man in the Iron Mask.

'My liege, you must hurry away from here. The King's

men are on their way. They have found out about your mother taking your place in the Bastille,' the man babbled. It was a horrible tale. Apparently, the Man in the Iron Mask's mother had had a full house at bingo, but another prisoner, Alfredo the Strangler, who was due to be hanged for tax evasion, accused her of cheating and challenged her to a fight.

As they struggled in the dimly lit cell, as they thrashed about in the straw, the mask-front flipped open and when Alfredo saw his opponent's face, he seemed to recognize it. The shock proved too much, and he died of heart failure. She attempted to cover up the accident by eating Alfredo and selling bits of him off to the other prisoners at an exorbitant price. This really annoyed them and one of them told the jailer what had transpired.

The wretched woman was stretched on the rack for half an hour, but remained silent. Hot oil was poured down her earholes, and still she spoke not a syllable. But when a priest whispered that if she didn't confess to everything he'd tell the newspapers how old she was, she revealed all, and what a story it was . . .

Before she had married the old King of France, she and Alfredo had toured the world as a tap-dancing partnership, sponsored by a Jesuit Building Society. Whilst performing in Peru, Alfredo had run away with an Inca town-crier, and formed a drag act specializing in Mexican Working Men's Clubs. She, poor, rejected woman that she was, became the mistress of a slave-dealer who bought her a bungalow in Cairo. Sweeping the sand off her shag-pile carpets eventually became too much for her to bear, and she started voting Liberal. One morning, she stole her lover's bank-book and absconded with all his savings, and made her way to France, posing as the Countess de la Plume. She met the King at a charity massacre of innocents, and the old fool fell for her, hook, line and sinker. In due course, she presented her royal husband with two sons, neither of them his, then tragedy struck. One night, after finding that he had an erection whilst on the lavatory, the King gave vent to a scream of pure joy. It quickly turned to a cry of terror as the weight of the enlarged organ pulled him down into the lavatory basin, where he drowned.

The two princes grew up lusty and healthy. One was a quiet, thoughtful, considerate youth, known in the palace as Frederick the Bore. The other, Louis, was a strong, violent, scheming young man, who eventually had his brother imprisoned in the Bastille, his face encased in an iron mask. Nobody knew why Louis did it; Frederick didn't even want to be King. All Louis would say, when taxed about it, was, 'Oh, I don't know . . . there's just something that pisses me off about our Fred.'

Now we were faced with capture. Fred looked at me. 'My friend', he said, 'we are in grave danger. Escape is impossible. Let us die with our swords in our hands.'

I drew my blade, he drew another blade, and he drew a better one than me, but then his pencil was sharper. Suddenly, and it might have been sooner, the King's soldiers ringed us with a circle of steel.

'By the hairs on Achilles' arse,' boomed forth the bearded officer, his pistol cocked in my direction. 'Look who we have caught in our net . . . none other than the Musketeer, Pierre Le Toq . . . a treacherous pig.'

'Fear not, my friends. You are not alone!' a strong voice rang out from a window-ledge above.

I risked a furtive glance, but the sunlight streaking through the dirt-caked glass made it difficult to see. Then a figure sprang down, and I swear by the phlegm of Lysander, I have never seen so swift an attack. Before I could lunge at the nearest trooper, our unknown saviour had cut down three of the King's men and gobbets of blood were flying all over the room.

Fred killed the bearded officer, but sustained a musket-ball wound in his left thigh. 'Go, my friend. Pursue those hounds. I will be fine. Go.' And with that, he fainted.

The bold slut Florence knelt by his side and ripped her bloomers into strips to bind the wound. (Having seen the state of her knickers, frankly, I'd have preferred to take my chances with good old-fashioned blood poisoning.)

I charged out into the street, my sword outstretched, but the King's men had gone, leaving only splashes of blood amid the heaps of horse-shit. There was no sign of the phantom swordsman either, only the Hunchback of Notre-Dame crouched in a nearby doorway, trying to invent a deaf aid. Was this my saviour? Surely not. No, he had vanished as mysteriously as he had appeared, and suddenly I knew beyond a shadow of a doubt that the mystery man was none other than the Blade of Passion. Musing over this strange turn of events, I beckoned to a rouged youth with a piss bottle and relieved myself, before mounting my horse and cantering to Madame Fifi's whorehouse.

For an hour I spent my ardour on the pale, rounded body of Janine, my favourite of all Madame Fifi's scrubbers. That painted harlot knew more positions than the author of the *Karma Sutra*. Finally, Janine emptied me, and my manhood shrank and withered. As she stood over me, I marvelled at her thighs like gammon steaks and the heated black bush hiding the slit of desire, the pendulous breasts, hanging like sacks of boiled Patna rice. Then I buried my face in her crotch and she knocked ten francs off the bill. That night, by the will of Apollo, I slumbered well, waking the next day to the familiar smells of Paris – freshly baked bread, stale pissoirs, cheap perfume and fresh horse-shit.

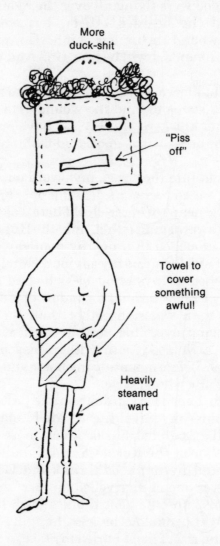

THE MAN IN THE IRON MASK!

Drawn on a fireman's collarbone during a heatwave — this sketch shows him coming out of a questionable sauna bath at a policeman's request.

PIERRE LE TOQ!

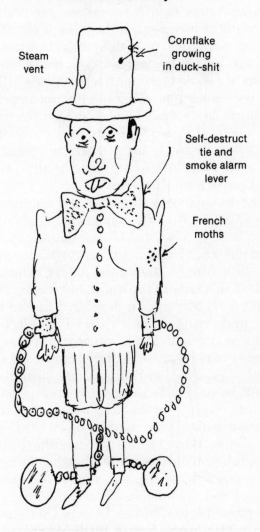

In chains for a library-card swindle in a Co-op annexe on behalf of a cruise director who took a bridging loan out on his foot.

I would have to be careful now, for word of my alliance with Fred would have spread throughout the capital, and King Louis would be calling for my head. The thought of the torture chambers made me shiver. I had seen men's eyes torn from their sockets, witnessed limbs sawn off living prisoners, and heard the terrified screams of people faced with a plumber's bill. By day, I hid in the catacombs (although I'm not struck on cats, I get a funny feline when I smell one), and by night, I stole away to a local bistro for bread and wine. On one such an occasion I saw, to my chagrin, a poster offering a large reward for the capture, dead or alive, of 'Pierre Le Toq – Traitor and Murderer!'

In the broadsheets there was no mention of Fred's escape from the Bastille, nor anything about his mum. It was a limbo period, and I knew not what to do. In fact, I knew not what I was doing, or, to put it another way, what was I doing? I knew not. I longed to nuzzle into the bare flesh of a lady of the night, but it was impossible. I couldn't trust anyone. In despair, I turned to drink to forget, and drank so much that I couldn't remember what I was trying to forget, and by that time, I couldn't remember why I was worrying about what I'd forgotten to remember. And so it was that, during one of my drunken bouts, I was dragged from my lodgings and taken into custody by the King's men, then thrown into a dungeon under the gendarmerie on the Pont du Niff. To my shame, I don't recall a thing. The first hint of my changed circumstances came when I woke upon a pallet of straw and saw my legs shackled to the wall. My heart sank . . . I was doomed.

Day passed into night as I lay in that stinking hole. The only light came from a tar-torch nailed to a stone buttress, and I thought myself alone, until one night I heard the rustle of straw and a hoarse voice crying, 'I don't care if I do go blind. It passes the time away.' At once I crawled towards the voice, as far as my chains would allow, and my fellow prisoner did likewise.

'Are you gay?' he whispered.

'No,' I whispered back.

'I never have any luck,' he muttered. He sounded irritated and I wanted to keep him talking, so I whispered: 'But I might try it one day.'

There was silence for a moment, then he replied, 'I'd make you very happy, chuck. I can cook a wonderful goulash and run up a pair of curtains in less than an hour.'

We got engaged in the morning when, by the light of a bright watery sun streaming through a small barred aperture, and bouncing off a guard's steel helmet, I saw my fiancé for the first time. He was wearing a crown of gold.

'Who are you?' I gasped in astonishment. He certainly cut a comic figure and no mistake. He was naked, and a long, matted beard hung to his waist, which helped to hide his wedding tackle. Like me, he was shackled to a wall, but on his head sat this crown.

'Sweetheart,' he simpered. 'I am the King of England, Richard the First, otherwise known as Richard the Lionheart, you silly goose.'

His was a strange tale indeed, and one that froze the blood in my veins, and the marrow in my bones. He'd come over to France on a day-trip with a friend who styled hair for a Northern ballet company and, within minutes of ordering a pot of herbal tea and an open sandwich, his brother John had had him flung into the Bastille without so much as a change of vest or his athlete's foot powder.

Time hung heavy in my prison and the food they served up was rotten. One day I threw my tin plate of worm-ridden broth at the jailer in anger, and I was dragged away and whipped until my back split and bled. A vast brute of a man rubbed salt into my wounds, but as he left he whispered, 'Take heart. The Blade of Passion will get you out.' Then he sang a nice song about a sheaf of wheat and a maiden with piles and, winking at me, clanged the dungeon door shut. I listened as his footsteps rang hollowly into the distance.

I heeded not the overtures of devotion from King Richard now, nor did I reply to the scented notes that he kept flirting across at me. I was going to be rescued from this living hell . . . but how? As I lay there, the dank air began to echo as prisoners in other dungeons groaned loudly. It was time for Quasimodo's weekly bell-ringing demonstrations.

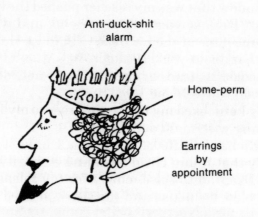

Anti-duck-shit alarm

Home-perm

Earrings by appointment

RICHARD THE LIONHEART!

Well-known imprisoned poof sketched by his friend Jerome coming out from a permissive hairdresser's bungalow. The only king with a pink castle and embroidered drawbridges, Richard had his soldiers in suspenders and roguish shorts for foot-drill. Very fond of braised frog's ankles on boiled lettuce — Richard was an idiot as well.

God's blood, the hunchback was boring! Bloody sodding bells clanging in your earholes for an hour! Damn it, they could have put a juggler on, or a jester – one of those new alternative jesters would have done – but bells? Great Jesus, how I hated them. King Richard pouted and asked for some flower-arranging classes, and then the straw started rustling fiercely again and I knew it wouldn't be too long before he had hand cramp.

All too soon, the guard unlocked my cell door and the hunchback entered, dragging a six-ton cast-iron bell behind him. The first boom deafened me and I clapped my hands over my ears. All of a sudden, the guard yelled, and an arrow bit deep into his guts. Dimly I saw the outline of an athletic man leap over the bell, and snatch the keys from the slain guard's tunic.

The shadow that was my rescuer pushed the keys into my hand. 'Release yourself, my friend, and when you are free, meet me at the La Belle Gigi in Le Havre.'

'But what about you?' I asked.

He shook his head, grinning. 'Fear not, dear ally, Quasimodo will help me.'

Swiftly I unlocked my fetters and rose to my feet. 'Are you coming with me, Your Majesty?'

King Richard sniffed. 'No, dearie. I have it on good authority that Robin Hood's holding a charity auction in West Drayton to raise money for my release.' With that, he blew me a kiss and the straw started rustling again.

Turning back to my rescuer, I wondered how Quasimodo was going to help the Blade of Passion to escape. The big oaf was just sat immobile inside his bell. I opened my mouth to speak, but the Blade waved me out of the cell, handing me a sword and saying, 'Don't forget . . . La Belle Gigi, Le Havre.' I nodded, impressed. Here was a man who obviously never did anything by Havres.

From within the stinking interior of the guard's room I heard rough shouts and the banging of wine pots on tables. As I crept past, clambering up the wet stone steps, I ran into a fat guard carrying a bucket of ale. I had no choice. With one mighty thrust, I ripped out his lungs, catching the body as it fell.

Once outside the barracks, I took no chances. Knowing that my appearance would cause comment, I dived at once into the thick waters of the Seine and swam down towards the Ile de la Cité. It was cold, so cold a brass monkey in Les Halles was advertising for a welder. I hauled myself on to the river bank and tried to get warm, but it was useless. God helped me, I swear, for a barge was drifting down the river, propelled by a pipe-smoking man. I dived back into the Seine and hurriedly swam towards it, and boarded the vessel. The man smoking the pipe never batted an eyelid.

'You'll find dry clothes below and some hot soup.' As the man spoke, he removed his woollen hat, and to my surprise I saw that it was the bold wench, Florence.

'By the red nipples of Circe,' I stammered. 'I thought you'd died.'

The harlot threw back her head and laughed. 'No, my dear Pierre. My hair is always this colour.' And with that somewhat odd remark, she felt my behind ... Honestly, if beauty was indeed skin deep, that woman was going through life inside out.

I tore myself from her questing hands and descended into the bowels of the barge, and bowels was right, for the craft stank of horse-shit, sheep-shit and cow-shit. As I stood there, holding my nose, a man in a green two-piece came out of the creaking gloom.

'Are you Captain Pierre Le Toq?' he asked in an effeminate voice. Two men stood on either side of him, both dressed as veiled bridesmaids.

When I nodded stiffly, the man said coyly, 'Well,

that's a good start, love,' and I thought, 'Right, that does it. Next time I'll nod my head.'

'Yes, I am Pierre Le Toq, late of the King's Musketeers, and, no, I don't know D'Artagnan.'

The man in green nodded solemnly. 'We know of your bravery and of your allegiance to Fred, the rightful King of France. But where is my King, Richard the Lionheart?'

The pieces were coming together now . . . this was obviously Robin Hood, but he didn't look Jewish. He must have read my mind because he sighed, sat down and read a passage from the Talmud. When he'd finished, we all chewed a bagel and Friar Tuck opened a packet of cashew nuts.

Of course, I told Robin Hood exactly where King Richard was, and how dangerous it would be to attempt to rescue the mincing old fool. Robin muttered something about leaving the old fart where he was until they'd counted up the money from the charity do in West Drayton.

After supping some home-made cider, I felt ill, and made my way to the rear of the barge in order to throw up. That action saved my life. As I vomited, my head hanging over the side, a shout went up and there was the sound of pistol-fire. The noise startled me, and I fell over the stern, but, fortunately, my pullover snagged on the rudder and helped keep my head above water. Meanwhile, from aboard the vessel, there came the sound of swordplay and fighting, and then the splash of bodies being heaved over the side. At one point Robin Hood floated past me.

'What's it like up there?' I panted.

'It's awful, pet,' he said, 'the noise, the people.'

Apparently, what had happened was, Maid Marian had come back to Sherwood, and found the shop unattended, and she'd thrown a wobbler. She knew Robin had a thing for King Richard, but thought he was getting over it, thanks to a daily dose of ginseng and a hormone tablet off Merlin. Anyway, she'd rented a galleon for the day and sailed across the Channel to bring Robin home. I had no desire to get involved in a domestic dispute so I turned away, just as Maid Marian grabbed her fellow out of the water and smacked him on the head.

I had to get to Le Havre, but how? I had no money to get to the coast and all France was baying for my blood. I became aware of the slut Florence beside me in the water.

Somehow, she managed to hoist me on to her back and, carrying me, swam quickly away . . . and I must confess, dear reader, that I was grateful for the respite. I must have fallen asleep, for when I came to my senses, Florrie and I were in the middle of the sea. What sea, I had no idea, but there was a lot of it and that was only on the top.

Florence said she was tiring, and at once I yelled, 'What, pray can I do to help?'

She half-turned in the middle of the breaststroke. 'Take my underpants down, Pierre, and give me one as I swim.'

I couldn't believe my ears . . . asking me to stick my manhood up her how's-your-father in the middle of a bloody ocean? Well, I ask you.

I shook my head. 'No way.'

'In that case,' she said, shrugging, 'we'll both drown.'

I knew she meant it, and made a desperate decision. Closing my eyes, I pulled down her odious drawers to reveal what must have been the biggest arse in Christendom. Honestly, she should have taken out harpoon insurance! After abandoning my pantaloons in the briny and somehow achieving a reasonable erection, I made love to Florence as she ploughed through the waves. She wasn't very impressed, however.

'I don't reckon much to your dick, Pierre,' she said,

mid-stroke. 'It is a little organ.'

This insult made me blazing mad, but I managed to remain calm while rocking back and forth on top of her. 'Sorry, Florence, but my organ has never played in such a big cathedral before.' Then she roared with the pleasure of her climax and I slid out gratefully, and fell asleep again.

'Wake up,' Florence shouted suddenly, and submerged. I rose to the surface of the sea, spluttering out salt water from my aching lungs.

'Where are we?' I shouted.

'I'm not sure,' she grunted, 'but there's a ship over yonder.'

True enough, by the will of Odin's scrotum, I saw a mighty ship with billowing sails, pitching in the swell and approaching Florence and me.

Strong hands pulled us out of the boiling sea, and while pigtailed sailors pumped water out of me, quite a few sailors looked after Florence. Judging by the expression on one man's face, it wasn't a banana she had in her mouth. Those lusty men of the sea gave me hot soup and warm clothes before taking me to see the captain . . . and as soon as I shook hands with him, I knew I was in the presence of none other than the English sea-hawk, Sir Francis Drake.

'How do, lad,' he said, tucking into a meat and potato pie. 'I'm Drake. Who are thee?'

When I told him, he seemed impressed and broke wind. 'Where are you bound, Captain?' I asked as he gave me a jar of pickles to open.

He scratched his ear with a quill pen. ''Ome, I reckon. There's nabbut about to plunder and I've a crew of right miserable sods.'

At that moment, a smartly dressed midshipman bounded into the cabin and reported that a ship was sailing towards them.

'Eh,' said Drake. ''Appen it will be my mate
Frobisher. 'E's a grand lad, tha knows, and damn good
at snooker. 'E's a fair clack on 'im, as well. I've never
seen him pissed yet.'

The midshipman saluted and said politely, 'It isn't
Frobisher, Captain. It's someone calling himself
Christopher Columbus.'

Drake hooked a bit of veal off a molar. 'I've heard of
him,' he said. 'Foreign chap. Used to knock about Genoa
with a bit of stuff called Mildred.'

I'd never heard of the place. 'Genoa?' I said.

'No,' Drake replied at once, 'but I heard she's got great
big tits.'

Chris Columbus turned out to be a true adventurer. He
made us all laugh with his tales of discovering America,
and I enjoyed a convivial evening, which finished off
with Drake singing the Bolton Football Club anthem
while old Columbus juggled with a pan of soot.

Round about dawn, gunfire woke me from a restless
sleep in my hammock. Drake came in, looking depressed.

'Sorry about the row, chuck,' he said as he fumbled
with his braces. 'Them bloody Spaniards have got up an
Armada and they're knocking hell out of our lads.' He
tutted and mashed a pot of tea.

'How are they taking it back in England, this Armada
business?' I said as I masticated a low-fat chipolata.

Drake looked at me and stroked his chin reflectively.
'Bit of a panic, I expect. Mind you, my press agent had
an idea summat might happen, so he hired a fellow who
looks like me to play bowls on Plymouth Ho! for an hour
every day. If the flaming Spaniards turn up, he's to keep
as cool as a cucumber, and then in years to come, owd
lad, I'll be a legend, and more than likely get a few bob
knocked off the price of a castle.'

Up on deck, cannons were booming and blood-heated
sailors were cursing and waving cutlasses. The leading

Spanish galleon sliced through the sea, getting into a position to give us a broadside or two, when suddenly I espied Florence waxing her legs in a wooden bucket. Apart from a hat, she was naked . . . God had heard my silent prayers. I took hold of her hand and shoved her over towards a rail, so that the Spaniards could see the naked frump. It did the trick. The firing stopped, and I heard someone on the poop-deck taking bets on whether it was a stranded porpoise or a badly ironed cricket-pitch cover.

Drake smiled and threw me a toffee, mouthing the words, 'Ta very much, cock.' Then he gave the order to open fire. His grapeshot raked the Spanish man o' war, and a roar went up as the foreign ship was blown to smithereens.

Florence was enjoying herself, and every time a Spanish survivor saw the size of her bum, he plunged back into the sea and drowned. The weather did the rest of the damage to the Armada. It was pelting it down, and the Spaniards hadn't got a mac between them.

A month later, Drake put me ashore at Plymouth and I caught a French packet . . . but the doctor said it would clear up eventually, if I didn't fiddle with it.

Ah, it was good to be back on French soil, and to smell that unmistakable aroma of good, honest, French horse-shit. With some of the money I'd won off Drake, playing strip-poker, I bought a second-hand sword, grew a moustache and dyed my hair black. I had to disguise myself, for France was in turmoil. In a playful mood, Pompadour had said, 'Give the buggers cake' and with that one single, stupid, ill-conceived remark, she had put the monarchy at risk. Now crowds were storming the palace gates, and the trams were on strike. The King's brother Fred had apparently vanished in Le Havre, and his mum had gone mad after being kissed by

a rabid duck in a giraffe's caravan. The Blade of
Passion hadn't done anything to excite, as it were, and
frankly it was a good thing the guillotine had been
given front-page news, because there wasn't a lot else to
gab about . . . and I had a herring in my pocket that was
beginning to smell.

Walking the boulevards at night was dangerous.
Footpads abounded, murderers stalked the unwary, and
there was talk of a poll tax. Twice, I had recourse to
unsheath my blade. I killed one robber with a single
thrust through his spleen, and rolled his body into the
Seine. Nobody would complain.

I grew bolder as I pranced about the city, for it soon
became clear that none of my previous acquaintances
had recognized me. Many times, the King's men
cantered past, but not one trooper stared in my
direction.

Then, one night, the Man in the Iron Mask, dear Fred,
sent for me. We met in a low billiard hall that straddled a
network of dark, mean streets near Montparnasse. The
place was full when I got there; in fact, there was a cue to
play snooker. We partook of a light meal of albatross
necks and swan's livers with penguin-foot sauce and
bread pudding for afters.

Fred was pleased to see me and I caught up with all
the latest news . . . King Richard was back home and
his brother Prince John had gone on his holidays to the
Isle of Man. Drake had sent me an invitation to sail
round the world with him, on a lap of honour to celebrate
his victory over the Armada and his new knighthood,
and Florence was pregnant.

'I am appalled by the revolution that is bringing
France to her knees,' said Fred. 'We must save the
aristocrats, otherwise the newspapers will have no one
to write about. And that is why I have secured the
services of a British secret agent, who is himself a

fairly decent aristocrat and worth a few bob. Pierre, my old and trusted friend, meet Albert.'

A tall, thin man stepped out from the shadows. His attire was immaculate and obviously very expensive . . . I noticed his spats came from Harrods.

'Charmed to meet you, old thing', the man simpered. His outstretched hand was limp and ponged of some sort of aromatic soap powder, but the most startling thing was his face. It was a mass of scarlet pimples. It looked like an advertisement for a set of coloured Lego.

'Good Heavens,' I stammered. 'What on earth is up with his boat-race?'

Fred was about to speak, but Albert gestured for him to remain silent.

'Mah dear old chum,' he lisped. 'When I was but a wisp of a thing, I was bitten on the lip by a deranged maniac with a grudge against BUPA. He claimed they'd given him blood poisoning while giving him a vasectomy during an earthquake.' He spoke softly, but with a sense of urgency, I felt. 'By the virtue of St Jerome, the pox has worked in my favour during these

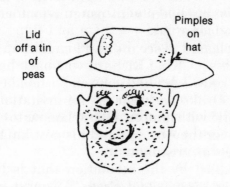

'PIMPLY AL'!

Sketched on the lavatory by his mother on his 21st birthday.

dark times, for people avoid me and I'm left to my own devices, and this is one of them.' With that, he pulled a plywood onion-grater from beneath his cloak. Fred poured out three tumblers of wine . . . an unusual vintage, it was a cross between Muscatel and Hock. It was Muck.

Apparently, Albert had been coming over to France on a regular basis, doing his bit for the posh, who were getting their heads lopped off. Because of his red, pimply face, he called himself the 'Scarlet Pimply Al', but of course, with the French having such awful sinuses, the title came out as the 'Scarlet Pimpernel'.

All that night we listened to his plans, and I quickly understood why the rightful King Fred had employed an Englishman, instead of a French chap from a Paris job centre.

As Albert explained, it was impossible to effect an escape for the doomed aristocrats; that sort of thing only happened in books. It was his intention to set up a dog-meat factory, putting in a tender for the bodies of the aristocrats to make the dog-meat, steal the severed heads from the tip in the Rue Royale, glue the heads back on the bodies and place them in prominent areas, so that the rebels would see them and think that the high-born buggers were immortal. The knowledge would put the fear of Christ up them and stop the executions. It was a brilliant ploy.

I hadn't heard from Florence in a while. Apparently, she had a good job standing outside a monastery with nothing on. Monks who had done their time took one look at her and signed on again.

Paris was a dangerous place to be. The peasants were encouraging the troops to desert, and soldiers were everywhere. The Blade of Passion had been at it again. The cool rogue held up one of the King's concubines in a chip shop, and had his way with her over a pan of batter before galloping away with her wristwatch and gold condom case. The Noise Abatement Society had told Quasimodo to shut up and leave the bells of Notre-Dame alone, but he was slobbering over some floosie called Esmeralda, and put in for more overtime instead. Things were in a right old pickle.

But for Fred, Albert and me, things were going very well indeed. Already we'd bought four bodies and found four suitable heads. I did the gluing and, even though I say it myself, and I am doing, I did a bloody good job . . . except once, when I stuck a head on back to front. But Albert was very nice about it. The peasants were as thick as pig-shit, he said, and would never notice. We left the body of the Comte du St Cluny in a pub, and the screams could be heard a mile away. Our plan was working. The trouble was, the guillotine operators were on a go-slow and the supply of bodies began to dry up. In order to save the aristocrats, Albert suggested that we three went out and killed a few, and that's when I realized that Scarlet Al was crackers.

I took Fred on one side and told him my fears, but it was useless – Fred and Albert had got engaged the day before, and Fred was as barmy as his new fiancé. There was nothing else for it: I drew my trusty sword and held the two silly sods at bay while I made my escape. Something had to be done. There and then, I made up my mind to tell the King what was going on. I knew that my life would be forfeit, but La Belle France, my mother country, came first . . . besides, I've got two feet, not four feet.

I galloped heavily towards the palace, trying to avoid the drunken peasants and rapacious troops who were despoiling the thoroughfares with flagrant sexual activities, queuing up for the winter sales and opening garden centres. Outside the palace, I dismounted and surrendered to the captain of the guard, a young fellow called Napoleon who'd been circumcised badly years ago, and had to keep scratching the tip of his willy with a stick which he kept inside his jacket.

'How do, Nap,' I said.

'Nice to see you again, Pierre,' he retorted, scratching feverishly. 'By the way, you're under arrest.'

They flung me into a filthy dungeon on the spot, ignoring my pleas for an audience with the King. I rotted away in that dank cell for a month, living only on rancid cheese, Co-op bread and Heinz broth.

One night they grabbed me while I slept and subjected me to the rack. How can I describe the agony of joints being pulled out of their sockets, the burning horror of flesh peeled away from tendons, and my despair at realizing I was now eight feet tall without shoes? Not content with all that, they then burnt me with hot irons and drenched me in boiling oil. I finally cracked when the swine brought in Florence, wearing only see-through knickers and a top hat. The prospect of having a leg-over with her in front of witnesses was too much, and I gave in, confessing to any damn thing. Eventually, shamed and humbled, I stood before my Monarch and related all that I knew.

The King was a frightened little fellow. Beads of sweat glistened on his royal brow. I wasn't surprised. Most of his best mates had scarpered as the revolution gained strength. He listened to my story, then said,'You lying git' and told them to take me to the Bastille. My heart sank, for my gamble had failed.

The smell in the prison was atrocious. How I longed for the odour of good clean horse-shit! Oddly enough, the jailers were extremely kind and the food wasn't half bad either. Instinctively, I knew I wouldn't be in the nick for long. Exactly three days later, the prison doors were battered down and triumphant peasants streamed in. I was hoisted up on their shoulders, not because of my heroism, but simply because word had got round that I'd given Florence one.

The next few weeks sped by in a bloody, confused whirl. Robespierre became governor, the King disappeared, heads lay everywhere. Marat was killed in the bath by Charlotte Corday because he wouldn't buy her a hand-driven dish-washer, and I was made supreme commander of the new republican army and given a villa in Cannes.

Life was good, but still one had to watch one's step . . . traitors lurked everywhere. To add to my worries, Florence was telling anybody who'd listen that her pregnancy was due to me. I became the laughing-stock of the new regime and behind my back the troops were calling me the Monster Shagger. Finally, Florence went on a market-place chat-show, and revealed to a stunned audience how I had committed a sexual assault on her in the sea . . . Robespierre sent for me.

I told him the truth – I had no option, my credibility had evaporated, as quickly as my dignity – in fact, an English theatrical agent had already offered me six weeks in Great Yarmouth, topping the bill on the end of a pier as a phallic jazz singer.

When I'd finished, Robespierre shuddered and said in an emotional voice, 'Jesus, son, you deserve the Legion of Honour, but alas . . . You must leave France for ever, otherwise this country of ours will start attracting the wrong sort of tourists. Florence has to go as well, I'm afraid. There are so many sketches of her in the nude that the government fears the birth rate will come to a full stop.' Then he halted and shouted to someone outside, 'Listen, Eiffel. Take that tower and stick it up your arse!'

Robespierre dismissed me with a handshake, a painting of his niece, a thousand francs and a one-way

ticket to Calais. But I quickly discovered that he had
other plans for my future.

As I crept out of the palace through a secret passage
and into a narrow street, six men in capes came at me,
brandishing swords. In silence they circled me like
predatory animals. My blade lunged at the nearest man,
and I felt the tremor of steel against steel as he parried
my thrust. Another sword ripped through my frogged
jacket, but I leapt back, and avoided injury. Back and
forth, we fought . . . clash upon clash of flashing metal,
gasping for breath. Fear pounded like drums in my
heart . . . I was tiring, and by now I'd been pricked three
or four times. One cut was quite deep, and I sensed blood
coursing down my flank. The end was nigh, I knew.
Then, out of the corner of my eye, I saw Quasimodo, the
Hunchback of Notre-Dame, at my side. Before I could
say anything, something happened that nearly took my
sanity away . . . his hump was moving! I watched,
stunned, as a dwarf slid down from under the hunchback's overcoat and launched into a dazzling display of
swordsmanship. Within two minutes, all six attackers
were dead, slaughtered by the fighting midget, and I
knew that once more I had been saved by the Blade of
Passion. Weak with fatigue and the loss of blood, I fell
down.

'Don't worry, Captain Le Toq,' my saviour said in a
well-educated voice. 'I have a degree in medicine. I'll
look after you.' Just before I passed out, I heard him say,
'Pick him up, Walter, and take him to Notre-Dame.'

Hours later I awoke to the sound of the great bells, and
my whole being shook with the shattering noise. The
dwarf soothed my brow and I noticed that my wounds
had been bandaged.

He smiled gently at me. 'How are you feeling, old
chap?'

I made a gesture to indicate that I felt much better,

and he handed me a cup of tea and a crumpet. The big
fat fellow, whom the midget had called Walter, was
hanging by his feet from a bell-clapper, blowing bubbles
in a clay pipe. 'Don't worry about Walter,' the dwarf
said, smiling at my expression. 'He's a head-banger but
harmless enough, unless he's playing with himself.'

Silly Walter did all the cooking, it seemed, and he
wasn't half bad at it, except he could never remember
what went with what. For instance, he would serve
steak with marmalade and cheese, and once he caused
me to vomit over the gargoyles when he cooked salmon
in an olive oil soup with a raw owl's egg. Actually, when
I think about it, living in that belfry was bloody awful,
and it wasn't just the bells. The pigeons shat everywhere.
My plumed hat was covered in it, and so was my cape;
even Walter looked as if he'd been white-washed. I was
getting deeply depressed and very randy. The nights
were hot, and I rarely slept because big Walter played
with himself inside the bell, and the boom of his hand
going up and down drove me bonkers.

The dwarf was away a lot on mysterious errands, but
to give him credit, he never bored me with tales of his
exploits. One night he announced that he was going to
make arrangements for us to flee to England. I must
admit I wasn't keen. Funny buggers, the English, and
the weather was crap. However, the only alternative
was death or exile to Holland, so stuff them and the
tulips, England it would have to be!

And so our plans were made. But we were forced to
wait for a signal that all was ready, and while we waited
we passed the time by playing Hunt the Ferret, and
Musical Chamber-pots. One evening, the dwarf told me
how he had begun his career as the Blade of Passion,
and I stayed awake all night long, listening to the most
gripping adventure since *Anne of Green Gables*.

READERS' JOKE COMPETITION

Why did the chicken cross the road? ... Because it was Thursday ... and Thursday is for perverts, or used to be when I was a young 'un!

(The above rib-tickler was submitted by a Mr Alvis Crustt, who is a former jitterbug with the Coal Board. Mr Crustt retired the same size that he started, but was found the wrong way round. He spent many years on his forehead looking for a gas leak in a two-way magazine-rack. His wife, who wishes to remain ridiculous, said that her husband hadn't felt well since losing an omelette through the steering wheel of a German canoe, but that his legs were roughly the same age. Our judges decided that, although the joke had been written down the side of a taxi mechanic, it was good enough to publish if the weather broke, and Mrs Crustt said they hadn't seen anyone who could write the Lord's Prayer on a peanut.)

NOW READ ON TO THE NEXT CHAPTER ...

THE DWARF'S STORY

The dwarf was the son of a wealthy swordmaker who couldn't make ends meet because he was taxed to the hilt. His mother christened him Quasimodo, although his father would have preferred Alf. His parents had so many other children, his father paid capital gains tax on his family allowance. In fact, there were so many wet nappies in the kitchen there was a rainbow in the lobby.

Right from the start it was obvious that Quasimodo was going to be a dwarf . . . little indications, like when he caught athlete's foot, he got it on the chin, and every time he hitched up his nappy he blindfolded himself. The other children made fun of him and the little lad grew up with no friends at all until Jean Leclerc, one of his father's employees, took an interest in him. Jean taught young Quasimodo the art of fencing, and it wasn't long before the small boy had outstripped his teacher. With money from his own pocket, Jean paid for Quasimodo to have lessons with a sword-master, one Georges du Pres. When he first espied the diminutive youth, du Pres laughed like a culvert, but changed his flippant attitude when he fenced with Quasimodo. This boy was superb! Before long, du Pres was devoted to Quasimodo . . . They once did the sabre dance, and it's still a sword point . . . still, they were epée days.

All this time, Quasimodo's parents had no inkling of

their tiny son's activities; they were under the impression that he was going to nightschool to learn stiltwalking. After one exhausting lesson, Georges du Pres threw down his foil, picked Quasimodo up in his arms and said, 'I cannot teach you any more, my son. You are the greatest swordsman I have ever encountered.'

That night Quasimodo dined with du Pres and his lovely daughter Elaine. She was so beautiful, her father had once arranged for her to be kidnapped so he could get a painting of her in the papers. She was the most exquisite creature the dwarf had ever set eyes on and that evening, over a plate of fried lark's tongues, he began to experience the discomfort of a full erection . . . Quasimodo was in love.

The next day, Georges du Pres had to go to Normandy because his father was being cremated (which was just as well because he was dead). Du Pres had told the crematorium that he'd be half an hour late, so they said they'd keep his father on a low light until he got there. Whilst his teacher was away, Quasimodo asked Elaine for a date and, purely in fun, she replied, 'One or two other boys have asked me out, but I'll put you on my short list.'

At this misguided reference to his size Quasimodo stormed off, raving mad. Elaine felt awful, so much so that she serenaded him under a full moon that night, with the song, 'Little Things Mean a Lot'. Quasimodo was so angry he sliced his mule's ears off.

No matter how hard she tried, Elaine couldn't help putting her foot in it. One day, on a picnic, a cheeky lout started throwing lumps of otter-shit at them. 'If you do that once more,' she said angrily, 'my friend Quasimodo here will black both your kneecaps.' It was an unfortunate remark to make, and Quasimodo ran the lout through and buried the body under a mound of sheep manure.

At last Quasimodo could take no more. He drew out his post office savings, packed a suitcase and set off for pastures new. But Elaine came running after him. 'Before you go, dear, dear Quasimodo, take away this memory of me.' With that, she opened her coat and the love-lorn midget saw that she was totally naked.

She lay down in the warm grass, holding out her arms. 'Come to me, possess me, Quasimodo. Take off your clothes. Remove everything, even your smalls.'

As soon as she said it, Elaine realized she had boobed again. Quasimodo's manhood shrank so far back it took a search party to find it again. It was the last straw, and Quasimodo turned his back on love, family and friends, and headed for Paris.

The huge, glittering city took his breath away . . . the magnificent buildings, the well-dressed citizens, the pomp, the sense of tradition and sophistication. He fell completely under its spell.

Harsh reality soon overshadowed him, however. Penniless, and without lodgings, he was forced to join the army of homeless in the city's catacombs. There, amongst the restless and lost legions, his hatred for the dissolute monarchy festered. With hunger gnawing at his very vitals and the cold, drilling winds of winter numbing his bones, Quasimodo found himself in the pit of despair. Half-delirious one night, he climbed on to a bridge and prepared to throw himself into the Seine . . .

Just as he was about to jump, a pair of arms caught him round the waist, and a voice in his ear said, 'Now, what do you think you're doing, little man? Surely things can't be that bad. Hmm . . . you could do with something to eat. I've seen more fat on a cold chip and that's a fact.

Quasimodo turned to see a burly man, well wrapped up in a thick top-coat and scarf. A big crimson nose hung over the top of the woollen scarf . . . it was the nose of a heavy drinker.

'Who are you, sir?' cried Quasimodo.

The burly man doffed his tall hat, revealing a head that was so bald, every time he went to a bowling alley, people put their fingers up his hooter.

'My name, little man, is René Claubert, and I am the proud owner of "Freaks Anonymous", the travelling show that is the talk of Europe.'

Rhino feather

Duck-shit

Dead thrush

2' — 6"

QUASIMODO!

'The Blade of Passion', classic sketch by Leonardo da Vinci's sister Iris, who glued orphans in a bakery for a man on a tam who kept trumpets.

Despite Quasimodo's protests, Claubert insisted on tucking him under one arm and carrying him off to a café in St Germain. There, the big man watched with kindly amusement as Quasimodo wolfed down the plate of food set before him. Two bottles of St Croix du Mont followed, and ere long the dwarf was sated, and he farted to show his appreciation. The smell was bloody awful and a wag handed Quasimodo a cork, saying, 'Stick that up your bum, midget.'

At once, Quasimodo leapt to his feet and faced the would-be comedian. 'If one of your cronies will hand me a sword, I shall show you some manners, you insolent popinjay.'

The whole café roared as Quasimodo issued this challenge, then a flashily attired man tossed him a sword and a hush filled the air.

The man who had started it all laughed, and drew his sword to smack Quasimodo with the flat of the blade. It was the last move he made. With one or two deft strokes, Quasimodo disarmed the man, cut his braces in half, ripped his shirt off and left him wearing just his vest and a rather peculiar truss. Claubert had never seen anything like it and decided he must have a truss too. Meanwhile, back to the plot . . . and there must be one, I suppose . . .

Claubert took one look at Quasimodo and smelt money with his outrageous snot valve. This dwarf must join his troupe.

That very evening, he gave Quasimodo a bed in the same room as the Lizard Man from Borneo and the Two-Headed Swamp Woman from Leyton Orient, and offered him a long-term contract of employment. Quasimodo need no persuasion. At last, he had found a niche for himself, with people who didn't snigger because he was short. He lost his virginity to the Two-Headed Swamp Woman after an evening on the

Guinness, and quickly became Claubert's biggest money-spinner. Night after night, he would issue a challenge to any young swordsman that he couldn't last more than a minute with him in a duel.

All the other oddballs in the show did their utmost to protect Quasimodo, and he loved them for it. There was Louise, the Bearded Lady, who used to eat live ducks through a string corset. There was the Great Rumbold, who sang under hot gravy whilst his auntie glued walnuts to a horse's penis. But the one Quasimodo was most fond of was called plainly Walter the Moron. All he did was let people belt him over the head with a slab of concrete or an iron pillar, then, while he lay in a coma, customers could knit his toes together and play scrabble for a bun. Walter and Quasimodo hit it off straightaway, and soon became great pals. The dwarf taught Walter things like how to breathe regular and count up to one, and big Walter would give Quasimodo donkey rides, then eat the donkey.

Meanwhile, business was booming. The Parisians queued up in their thousands to see the show, and René Claubert was pulling in the profits. The crowds gasped as the freaks went through their paces. The Two-Headed Swamp Woman danced on a pair of cork trousers that had been lined with hot pitch, and while she played a banjo, her two heads whistled 'Dixie' in harmony. Agog, the crowds roared for more. The Man with the Alligator's Genitals really stunned the ladies in particular, and two nuns followed him back to his water tank with an extraordinary proposition. But when little Quasimodo was carried on stage by Walter the Moron, a hush spread through the audience, and tall, menacing men edged closer. For Quasimodo's reputation had spread far and wide and every hot-blooded buck wanted to test his steel against the midget.

The first challenge was accepted by a six-foot Zulu in

a made-to-measure trilby and horse blanket. He lasted
fifteen seconds before the talented shrimp disarmed and
humiliated the proud warrior, by making him sing:

> There once was an old Portuguese,
> Who slowly sank down to his knees
> And said, 'It would be bliss
> If you got hold of this . . .
> But for God's Sake, be careful of these!'

Little did Quasimodo know how closely his performance was being observed by one of the King's secret
agents, Juan Le Bond . . . and, being a Bond, his work
was at a premium. Juan had worked for a time in the
Bank of England at Christmas as a Mint Spy. In the
Sûreté, he was code-named '003', which meant he was
entitled to strangle hernias and wear leggings in an
avalanche. That night, Bond crept away and mounted
his horse. (In those days the police couldn't touch you
for it, and horses often wore a smile.)

The King listened to Le Bond's story intently.'You
think this midget is the little swine who has roused the
peasants to revolt?' he said.

Bond nodded. 'I do, sire. His expertise with a sword is
uncanny. There is no soldier in your army who can
match him.' Just then, Madame de Pompadour walked
into the salon with a small, red-haired, freckled woman
in a bonnet and shawl.

'Permit me to introduce Mary, Queen of Scots,'
Pompadour said very grandly.

'Not now, love,' the King replied, a hint of irritation in
his voice. 'I'm busy. Come back later and we'll have a
brew.'

Pompadour waved her fan vigorously. 'No, no, you
misconstrue,' she said.

'I know,' the King said. 'I always do in the warm
weather.'

Madame de Pompadour stamped her foot and sent someone to post it. 'You don't understand. Mary knows a man who can beat the dwarf.' And with that, she hopped on to a window-sill.

'Speak, woman,' the King said. 'I'm all ears.' (It's a well-known historical fact that the King of France had three ears: a left one, a right one and a wild front ear . . . It's not a bad joke to use on kids.)

Mary curtsied, cleared her throat and spoke thus: 'Octa noo, mah wee man. Naw, ye noo och tat doo noo.'

The King looked at her and nodded his head gravely before turning to Pompadour, saying, 'What the bloody hell did she say?'

Fortunately, Pompadour knew a lot about the Scotch . . . she was often legless on it. She sat on the King's knee and whispered, 'She knows a Highlander who's never been defeated with a claymore, and she says that if you help Bonnie Prince Charlie grab the throne of England, she'll get the Highlander to kill the dwarf.'

'All right, What's this fellow's name?'

Pompadour put her hip-flask back under her wig and said, 'His name is Rob Roy MacGregor.'

A cunning alliance was forged that night, and Mary, Queen of Scots bought them all a fish supper.

Rob Roy lived in digs in Doncaster and there wasn't a lot to do round there. His mistress had gone on a coach trip to Colwyn Bay and there was nobody in the place worth fighting, so he spent a lot of time at the pictures. It came as a great relief when a French messenger handed him a note asking him to nip across the Channel and put paid to the fencing midget.

He reached France two days later, after a nice enough trip with Thomas Cook and Company, and made straight for the hostel run by the Brittany branch of Social Securities, where Mary, Queen of Scots was staying until a throne could be found for her. (Actually, as history would point out, she wanted the English throne for herself. Bonnie Prince Charlie couldn't have cared less about it; he was happy with his ceramics and the cute blond boy in the Methodist church choir.)

It was nine-fifteen at night when MacGregor reached the edge of the stage. Quasimodo had just beaten his fiftieth challenger, and he was knackered.

'Well, that's it for tonight,' boomed the jovial Claubert. 'Come back tomorrow, folks . . .' He never finished the sentence, for at that precise moment, MacGregor jumped on to the stage, shouting, 'Octa noo, mah wee man. Naw, ye noo och tat doo noo.'

'Send for Pompadour,' Claubert said, 'I can't understand one sodding word.'

Breathing heavily, because Claubert was stood on his chest, Quasimodo said, 'I know what he said. I understand the language . . . I once played the Glasgow Pavilion on a split week.'

The crowd tensed and the sharp stench of fear rose high into the black night. The two men stared at each other, knowing that death would come to one of them. The bloodthirsty crowd knew it too, and the sale of hamburgers without onions shot up.

Parry, thrust, thrust and parry, the combat waged to and fro, the weapons catching slivers of light off the rush lamps. One minute the great claymore seemed to be master, then the slender, chased Toledo blade that was part of Quasimodo would flicker like a fiery dancer and send the claymore reeling back.

For over an hour the two men fought, and it looked as if there would be extra time when suddenly Quasimodo shouted, 'Look! There's a penny on the floor.' It did the trick and as MacGregor bent down to look, Quasimodo ran the mighty Scotsman through. MacGregor fell to the floor, uttering the never-to-be-forgotten words: 'Octa noo, mah wee man. Naw, ye noo och tat doo noo.'

Holding his dripping sword aloft, Quasimodo's voice rang out. 'Rob Roy MacGregor, I salute you for being a brave warrior. And now, dear friends, lift him up out of the horse-shit.'

Claubert shook his head and blew his huge nose loudly into his hankie. 'Nay, nay, Quasimodo, let him be. He's the sort of chap who would have wanted to die, or at least go through the motions.'

In his heart of hearts, Claubert knew that Quasimodo would have to leave the freak show now. MacGregor's death would have been noticed, and danger lurked everywhere. Sadly he threw a party for little man, and presented him with a cuckoo clock on HP, and the cast sang, 'For he's a jolly good midget' while tears ran unchecked down their faces . . .

And so Quasimodo waved goodbye to the wonderful Claubert and all his new friends. He didn't want to go, but he knew that, if he stayed, their lives would be in jeopardy.

On he trudged, down the moonlit path that would take him to the main road from Paris to Orléans. He didn't know where he was going, nor did he care. Just then, he heard a mighty thud and, turning, he saw Walter the Moron behind him. The big fool had tripped over a bullock.

'Why are you following me, Walt?' Quasimodo asked, as the daft giant picked a set of horns from his dentures. Walter stood up, wringing his hands, and when Quasimodo answered, it was an offer for a time-share on a flat.

'I'm asking you, Walt, why are you following me?' Quasimodo spoke sharply.

'Becos you are my pal, Quasie,' replied the idiot. 'I want to be with you aaalll the time. Give me a sweetie.'

With a deep sigh, Quasimodo handed over one of the

mint imperials he kept up his armpit in a leather purse, in case of emergencies.

'Now look here, Walter,' he said. 'You'll have to go back to the others. There's no place for a genuine head-banger around here, unless you're a learner driver.'

On hearing this, the cretin uprooted a tree and started hitting himself on the head with it. 'You don't like me any more, do you, Quasie?'

Quasimodo couldn't leave the lunatic on his own, and it occurred to him that the fool's great strength might just come in handy. So he beckoned barmy Walter to follow him, and off they went together.

They slept under a bush that night, and as they slaked their thirst at a stream, Walter asked Quasimodo to tell him what girls were for. When Quasimodo had explained, Walter asked for one to play with. Curtly the midget said no. Upon which, at once, Walter lay down, drumming his heels on the grass and shouting, 'Get me a girl, Quasie. I want one to hold and to bounce up and down. Get me one, Quasie. Please.'

Quasimodo had to put up with this for a whole week. He tried to calm down the big clod by showing him dirty postcards, but Walter was insistent. He wanted a real girl. In desperation, the midget stole down to a village one night and found a council-run brothel. He explained the situation to a most agreeable madam, and she said that, for an extra bob or two, she'd relieve the giant herself as she had had lots of experience with imbeciles. As she put it, 'Problematically, it is a transverse malady that creates a highly inflammatory sexual necessity brought on by the state of dithyrambic in the vertiginous imbalance of the cranial fluidity –' she handed Quasimodo another almond slice and a Garibaldi biscuit – 'The futility of repressed emotive desires, added invariably to inadequate genitalia, becomes a corybantic maelstrom, and cessates only in tragedy.' As they chatted, Quasimodo and the good madam walked down the tree-lined path to where Walter sat, strangling a moose.

'You may leave us now, little man,' the madam assured Quasimodo. 'Your friend will be safe in my hands. As I said before, he may be a big man but ten to one he has a small penis.' With that, the madam took Walter by the hand and they vanished into some shrubbery. There was a short silence, then the sound of clothing being ripped off could be heard. Quasimodo tried to close his mind to what was taking place, but suddenly he heard the madam shout in a voice full of wonder, 'Bloody hell, Walter, does it bite?' This was followed by some 'Oohs' and 'Aahhs', then the madam's voice rang out deep and clear, 'Little man? Do you remember what I said about big men having small bits? I was wrong, thank God.'

When Quasimodo awoke, it was to the sound of female voices. To his amazement, he saw a long queue of women standing in front of the shrubbery. Sword in hand, he leapt to his feet. 'You can put that away,' said the madam. 'I've brought along a few girls for Walter.'

Quasimodo couldn't believe his eyes. 'What on earth is going on, woman?' he demanded.

She lit her pipe deliberately. 'In all my years, I've never seen a cock as big as your mate's.' She puffed contentedly, then went on, 'Fluoride in the water round here causes male droop, and the girls in the village haven't sat on a hard one for ages, so I thought I'd give 'em a treat. Besides, at twenty francs a go, it's a tidy little business, if you see what I mean.'

Quasimodo finally managed to smuggle Walter away from the never-ending line of rapacious ladies just before the coming of dawn. The odd couple crept through the dew, then stole a horse and cart in order to

False hump with
serving-hatch and
holiday slides

Built-in Weetabix

Korean
Rolex

WALTER THE MORON!

A sketch of the famous idiot trying to remember his
name during a Druid staff dance — his death mask
can be seen in a Cork warehouse under a short
priest's foot.

effect an escape. Walter couldn't stop drooling, and he rambled on and on about his 'living dollies': 'I wanna hug them and pat them.' It was getting on Quasimodo's nerves and he fervently wished he'd never brought the mindless berk with him. He was soon to change his tune, however. Because of MacGregor's defeat at the hands of the dwarf, relations between France and Scotland had cooled somewhat and there wasn't a bloater to be seen in all France.

The word was: 'Find and destroy Quasimodo!' Large rewards had been offered for his capture, dead or alive. When the women whom Walter had entertained so well were interrogated by the King's men, they all said the same thing: 'Yes, there was a midget knocking about, but sod him. Bring back the fellow with the anaconda willy.' This totally confused the King's men and three of them caught dysentery.

Then it happened – the incident that was to create the 'Blade of Passion'. Just when they thought they were safe, Quasimodo found himself surrounded by a troop of the King's loyal musketeers. He and Walter had gone into an inn to eat. They had no money, but all Quasimodo had to do was issue a challenge to any man there who thought he had a bigger dick than Walter. They'd already won hands down three times before, by at least seven inches. Sadly, on one occasion, a fishmonger with a fair reputation down below had lost with ill-grace and then got fed up, overdosed on health salts and fizzed to death. On this night, however, all seemed well. Later on, Quasimodo would admit that he should have known something was up, because the inn was empty except for the landlord who was naked apart from his socks, carrying a notice which read:

There was an old man from Bengal
Who had a mathematical ball.
The square root of its weight
Minus penis plus eight,
Equals $\frac{5}{8}$ or $\frac{3}{5}$s of f— all.

The words were written in a rare Peruvian script and could only be read at a distance of ten yards if the river was in the right direction.

Suddenly, the King's men swarmed down from the minstrels' gallery on ropes, and Quasimodo had to fight for his life. He killed many with his flashing blade, but then more troops arrived, lured by the offer of early retirement and a decent demob suit. Quasimodo was forced further back and his little arm was tired. All seemed lost, when he heard Walter singing in the lavatory. With one last determined effort, he slew five more soldiers and retreated into the loo. Big Wally was having a pee in the tin trough and, without thinking, Quasimodo jumped on his friend's back and inside his cardigan and hid. When the soldiers dashed in they shook their heads in disbelief. Quasimodo had vanished. An officer came in, pistol cocked at the ready. 'Well, where is he?' he snarled.

One of the soldiers shrugged his shoulders. 'He has vanished, sir. The only person in here is this giant hunchback washing a pig in the trough.'

The officer peered under Walter's arm and said in an awed whisper, 'Christ! If I had one like that, I'd either be in a circus or giving one to every bugger.' Then he made his men form an orderly queue so they could all have a peep at Walter's thingy. Afterwards, the lads left somewhat thoughtfully.

When the soldiers had gone, Quasimodo clambered down and Walter said, 'Hello, little pal. I've just had a wee-wee. Can I have another living dolly?'

Quasimodo shook his head. 'Not now, Walter. Just put it away and let's get out of here.'

Gingerly, and with Walter rumbling behind him, Quasimodo crept from the inn into the night. There was no need for caution, since all the King's Musketeers were stood on the front lawn, tape-measures in their hands and underpants round their ankles. They all seemed a bit put out, and they were calling one sergeant 'Alice'.

Reasoning that they wouldn't be noticed in a big city, Walter and Quasimodo retraced their steps. They reached Paris five days later.

As they trudged past Notre-Dame, *en route* to an auberge in the district of Odéon, they passed a priest. He looked at Walter and said, 'By the rising of Jesus, you're a big lad. How would you like to become a bell-ringer? I'm a bit stuck, you see. The fellow who normally does it has been burnt at the stake.'

Taking the chance that the good and saintly man hadn't really noticed him, Quasimodo jumped up Walter's cardigan at once and spoke, manipulating Wally's jaws to make it look as if it was he who spoke, if you see what I mean. At any rate, it appeared to work and the priest took Walter up to the belfry and never once asked for his P45.

It was an ideal hiding-place, up there in the belfry, and during the days that followed, Quasimodo furnished it with a studio couch, a cocktail cabinet and a shag-pile carpet.

Walter took to ringing the bells a treat, and to keep him happy Quasimodo smuggled a few girls in from time to time, for Walter to hug and bounce and all that sort of thing. For their part, the girls loved it, and after seeing the size of Walter's penis, Quasimodo knew their hiding-place would remain a well-kept secret.

And yet the midget was restless. The fight for liberty raged within his heart as daily he witnessed the injustices heaped upon the long-suffering populace by the minions of a dissolute monarchy . . . and the heaps were getting bigger.

Then, whilst smacking Walter on the head with a fireside onyx water-clock one evening, Quasimodo hit on the idea of calling himself the Blade of Passion. It was a decision that was to transform his life.

Three nights later, he deliberately broke wind at the opera, during a quiet bit in the first half of *Tosca*, then blamed it on the mistress of a high-ranking flute wholesaler when the smell made the King throw up in his bowl of cornflakes.

At once, the King's personal bodyguards drew their swords and clattered up to the balcony, where Quasimodo was sitting. But the midget slew them before anyone had time to sing 'Old Man River' and raced down to the foyer, where Walter waited. Quickly the midget unfurled a rope ladder, climbed up it and hung on to his big friend's vest, thus making his escape.

Within a month the Blade of Passion was the talk of France and parts of North Acton. Many people felt grateful to him for seeing off so many of the King's men, although a lot of conscripts who'd only got a few more months to do wished he'd give over.

Not for a second did anyone suspect that the hump up Walter's jumper might be little Quasimodo. In fact, because of his ability to vanish as if into thin air, people began to think the Blade of Passion was some sort of magician.

That was the narrative told to me, Pierre Le Toq, by the Blade himself, as we sat up in the belfry of Notre-Dame. I remember the night well . . . we dined on a supper of stewed veal in a thick crust of unleavened bread,

followed by a lightly ironed pancake on a bed of freshly
stitched truffles and boiled lung of thrush, all prepared
by the idiot Walter inside his iced apron. It was
delicious.

Time passed, and Quasimodo sensed that I was
getting bored with life in the belfry, so one night he and I
climbed up Wally's back and went for a night out in the
Place Pigalle. There was an amplitude of crumpet in the
clubs, and a well-built tart with a neck-brace did me a
favour against the door of a bookmaker's shop down a
side-street. Quasimodo didn't bother looking for a leg-
over, and I wondered if he was a bit embarrassed, sort
of. Big Walter had a smashing time in a pet shop,
bouncing dogs off the walls and sucking the bones from
out of a live swan.

Then, as we made our way home, Quasimodo and I
sitting up Walter's vest, playing our mouth organs, we
were stopped by the night patrol.

'Why, it's the bell-ringer,' I heard a patrolman shout.
'Let's have some sport with the idiot.'

Stealthily, Quasimodo drew his sword, and I cocked
my pistol.

'Go away,' Walter said. 'Or my pals on my back will
spank you.'

We heard the patrolmen roar with laughter. 'By the
beard of the prophet! I do believe he's going to hit us
with his hump!'

A moment later, we had slid down on Walter's braces,
and Quasimodo had pierced an astonished soldier
through the heart while I fired point-blank into the face
of another. What we hadn't anticipated was the size of
the patrol. I counted six hundred of them on foot and
God only knows how many on horseback. There were at
least three regiments of lancers with a squadron of
hussars and mounted artillery in support. Walter said
he thought he saw a ship of the line coming round the

corner, but you can't take any bloody notice of Walter. I did see a full battalion of pikemen, though, and, at a rough estimate, three camel corps and a fellow from the Foreign Legion with his wife. (Much later on, we learned that the patrol that night had numbered over half a million soldiers and some bricklayers who had been rained off from a housing estate.)

The news that the Blade of Passion had been captured swept throughout Europe like wildfire, and the report that he had used a bell-ringer's vest to hide in was greeted with so much amusement, there was talk of a sit-com being done about it.

There was no doubt about it, we three were in grave peril and our situation was horrific. From the night of our being taken prisoner, we had been thrown into the Bastille and chained hand and foot. There was quite a bit in the Sunday papers about me, and someone had done a cartoon of Walter the Moron, for the *Tatler*.

In fact, Big Wally rather liked being in prison. There was never a shortage of mice for him to bounce and nobody bothered if he peed up a wall. I, however, had a deep feeling of foreboding that we would not be left in the Bastille for long. I felt sure that, once public opinion had settled down, the authorities would whisk us away to a place even more secure, where eventually we would rot and be forgotten, rather like owning a rest-home in Lyme Regis.

My forebodings were absolutely correct. Two weeks later, Quasimodo, Walter and I were dragged out of our foul dungeon and taken on board a prison ship. And as the cold sea wind drilled into our shackled bodies, fear gripped my bowels. We were going to be incarcerated in the Château d'If, and there was no escape from that foul place.

It was dawn when the prison ship pitched and tossed

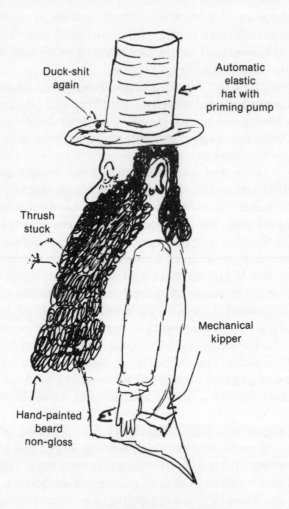

Duck-shit again

Automatic elastic hat with priming pump

Thrush stuck

Mechanical kipper

Hand-painted beard non-gloss

EDMOND DANTÉS
Sketch taken under the floor of a mushroom farm by a comedian doing a pantomine in a government-sponsored cemetery.

into the rugged harbour nearest to the Château d'If, but we captives nearly even glimpsed the skyline. We were dragged down steep stone steps into a reeking gloom that held the stink of hell itself.

I was hurled into a cell by myself, and manacled to the wall by a rusty chain round my waist. The first thing I did was to tap on the walls like they all do in prison stories, but the only message I received was, 'Shut up! We're playing bridge.'

It took me a year to chisel out a doorway in the stone wall of my cell, and it did look nice against the Doric-style pillars that I'd hewn out on either side of the firegrate I'd knocked up, with the aid of a diagram I'd seen in an Easter copy of *Reader's Digest*. I held a topping-out party, and it was good to see Walter and Quasimodo again. The biggest surprise was to find that Robin Hood the Jewish outlaw, Fred the one-time Man in the Iron Mask and, of all people, spotty old Pimply Al were in there too! Edmond Dantés ran whist-drives and held staff dances for a charity organization who raised funds for the heavily withered.

After a while, somebody took my chains off and led me to the swimming-pool near a health food bar. When I asked if they'd ever thought of escaping, Edmond Dantés went pale.

'Not bloody likely, Pierre,' he said. And, as time wore on, I had to admit that conditions in the Château weren't at all bad, although the smoked salmon they served up was often a bit sweaty, and the caterers hadn't a clue how to baste an ox in cranberry juice. However, apart from these sufferings, life was pretty good . . . until one of our jailers came to tell us that Florence, now heavy with child, had been kidnapped by gypsies. From all accounts, they'd demanded ten thousand francs in ransom money for her, but at the finish they'd offered to pay it themselves. The jailer said that Florence was coming to the Château d'If as a window-cleaner and part-time research engineer ... That was all we needed to hear. Plans were made at once for a mass escape.

READERS' JOKE COMPETITION

Why did the chicken who was perverted cross the road on a Thursday? ... Because it fancied stuffing something at the 'weak end'.

The above shaft of unexpurgated fun was sent in by Mr Casper Trump, whose niece claims to be the real Prince Philip, and is quite prepared to shave to prove it. Mr Trump has never asked for a family allowance rebate and can't go to the lavatory if there's an R in the month. Mr Trump worked for many years modelling windmills out of soot, but retired when he lost his balance.)

BACK TO THE PLOT ...

THE TESTIMONY OF
LOUIS BOVARY

Before I throw myself on to the mercy of the reader, I feel it is only fair to give you some background on myself, should you consider suing the publisher.

For most of my life, I lived in the sweet little village of Ruffe-on-the Ole. This placid hamlet, lying at the foot of Mont Blanc, is so far off the beaten track, Dracula got in for the Liberals. The natives were simple folk and took it in turn to be village idiot. My father was the local blacksmith and my mother worked for him. She was very strong and when the shoes were ready, she'd hand Daddy the horse.

I did quite well at school and I loved poetry in particular. This verse still reminds me of my childhood:

> There was a young sailor named Bates
> Who danced the last waltz on his skates,
> But he fell on his cutlass
> Which rendered him nutless,
> And the poor sod's now useless on dates.

Most of my school chums thought I was girlish, mainly because I was shy and wore suspenders. But I didn't care ... I had my poetry and the rolling fields and soaring hills to spend endless hours exploring. My wonderful childhood came to a horrible end when my father went quite mad and shod my mother's feet with horseshoes, then broke into a zoo and ate an elephant. They took poor Daddy away in a long basket and Mummy entered a horse auction and was bought by an Arab for stud purposes.

As for me, I was sent to Paris to live with my grandmother and, oh, how I hated the bustling city and the constant smell of horse-shit ... sorry, I mean, manure.

Dear grandmother did her best to give me a good home, but she was ninety-eight years old and inclined, I'm afraid, to be lazy. On one occasion, I had to shout three times before she came up and dressed me. She had a decent job as a bouncer in a gambling club, but flatly refused to take on another type of employment to earn an extra bob or two, and we fell out over it, not unnaturally.

Finally, she agreed to go kick-boxing, while I stayed at home, alone and in a state of bliss, for now I was a poet.

> From the depths of the crypt in St Giles
> Came a scream that resounded for miles.
> Said the vicar, 'Good gracious,
> Has Father Ignatius
> Forgotten the Bishop has piles?'

I sold that, my first poem, to a brewery rep and he still keeps in touch.

As the years passed, I became one of the café dwellers on the Left Bank, and my reputation as a poet and Bohemian grew. Grandmother retired from kick-boxing, and was now promoting non-stick rhubarb for a Mormon socialist. I didn't see a lot of her, which suited me, because she'd told a friend of hers that she thought my poetry was crap, and on one Whit Sunday she'd set fire to my suspenders.

I've never been one for politics, but even my artistic soul was outraged by all the noble heads lying on the city rubbish-tips. Frankly, I found the revolutionary leaders very common and such goings-on made me shudder.

It was at this time that I met the painter Van Gogh. He was a nice enough chap, and if you told him something it went in one ear and stayed there. We used to meet in the Café Royale, under a viaduct in a blouse factory. The beer was half-price if you walked in backwards with a box of dominoes. It was a good gimmick and the place was always full of interesting people.

In that gay café I met and fell in love with Nina, a black-haired beauty from Amsterdam. Our love was purely platonic, and I still recall with tearful nostalgia the nights we roamed the narrow streets of old Paris, holding hands in the soft moonglow that bathed the city skyline. She was such fun to be with. I adored the way she'd pull her purple knickers over her head and pretend to be a plum. Once she took me to a concert and, to my astonishment, she got on to the stage and did a stand-up comedy act . . .

> 'Good evening. I wouldn't say my room is small, but if I put my shoes out to be cleaned, I have to leave my feet inside them . . . You don't believe me? Listen, pal, the fleas on the dog's back daren't jump in case of concussion . . . If I talk to myself one of me has to go outside to reply . . .
>
> My husband is so ugly, when he went for a swim in Loch Ness, the monster got out and picketed the lake . . . Thank you and good night.'

Nina did make me laugh, although I'd already heard
most of the jokes off a pedlar who'd been on *New Faces*.
Oddly enough, the audience weren't enthusiastic, and I
heard the café manager telling her to piss off. Nina
ignored him, and took a curtain call, a watch and a roll
of lino.

I was besotted with her. I could see no flaws in her
whatsoever, despite the fact that she grew facial hair
whenever there was a full moon. We moved into a small
apartment together and even though several people
were found with their throats torn out, I didn't think too
much about it until she started going to the zoo to chat to
a wolf.

We hadn't had sex at that point, so it came as a shock
when Nina pointed to a red setter mounting a bitch and
said, 'We ought to do it that way.'

Like an idiot, I replied, 'What a good idea, but we'll
have to find a street where nobody knows us.' She
seemed to go off the idea after that remark, and didn't
speak to me for the rest of the night.

I'd just composed my latest verse in tribute to
Robespierre's leadership and he'd given me a few bob to
put in the post office. The poem was printed in a weekly
broadsheet and was well received. In fact, it still ranks
as one of the finest pieces of verse to come out of France.

> It's not the size
> That does attract the flies,
> It's the gyppo round the rim.

Then the bombshell occurred, a terrible event that
was to change the course of my life. During the recent
full moon, Nina had apparently waited patiently at a
bus-stop whilst her facial hair and fangs grew, and then
she'd tried to chew the Adam's apple off a friend of
Robespierre. The victim, a woman, had contrived to get

away and Nina was arrested in a park, chasing some Brownies. The court case was a sensation. Nina's name was linked to mine, and a man sailed over from the *News of the World* with some money in an envelope.

My darling was brought up before the Citizens' Tribunal and charged with murder, bestiality and fouling the pavements, which was a hoot, when you consider that the Paris streets were three inches deep in horse-shit. She looked guilty in the dock, and there was talk of her being spayed and her licence being endorsed.

I attended the hearing every day, for did I not love the damsel? But as the trial drew to a close, it was obvious that everybody from the judges down to the clerks thought her guilty. The shadow of death at the hands of a vet seemed the logical conclusion, until the day Nina stood up and demanded to be heard.

'Fellow citizens of my beloved France, yes, I am guilty of the charges brought against me, and yes, I am a werewolf, and yes, I have killed.' The courtroom was as quiet as a flag day in Aberdeen while she spoke. 'To end my life would be a merciful act, because, not only am I a monster, but the man I loved betrayed me and I'm overdrawn at the bank.' She stopped speaking, pulled out an Aztec clarinet and played a piano concerto. Then, with her index finger quivering in my direction, the harpy spat out the words that were to damn me for ever . . . 'And there sits the man who betrayed me . . . Louis Bovary.'

I could not believe my ears, sweet reader, and Van Gogh couldn't believe his one either. Nina, the furnace of my desires, was lying through her fillings. But why? As these and many other questions darted back and forth across my mind, Nina continued her damning tirade . . .

'There were times, while I lay in his arms, when I begged him to have me seen to, or at least to buy me a tin of Chum, but no, he said he preferred me half-animal because it aroused him.'

I could not believe the lies she poured forth, and I was getting a few peculiar looks, I can tell you . . . especially from a spinster who kept shaking a dog lead and a bit of paper with her address written on it.

All at once, the tide of opinion turned in Nina's favour. Cries of, 'Trust a bloody man!' and 'Hang the bastard' were quickly followed by a woman burning her steel-ribbed breast-holder and Flemish knicker-gusset, and I had to be hustled away for my own safety.

An hour later came the court's verdict. Nina was to be exiled to the forest, and if she happened to mate with a wolf, the kids would have to be raised as good Catholics. It wasn't a prison sentence at all! Some foreigner called Disney had turned the forest into a holiday camp, and Nina would obviously finish up as a resident guide-dog for the blind or an official at Cruft's.

I came out of the scandal very badly. I was sent to Coventry, hated it, but didn't mind Birmingham. My poetry stopped selling, and my so-called Bohemian friends turned their backs on me. My credit in the Left Bank cafés had run out.

Once I was attacked by a gang of effeminate men who threw me to the ground and styled my hair differently. I stumbled home, shocked and afraid that they'd used too much lacquer and, as I turned the key in the door of my apartment, two large men stepped from the shadows and grabbed me. One of them said sternly, 'Are you the poet Louis Bovary? I nodded. 'Did you pen this verse?' he went on.

I peered through the gloom at the sheet of foolscap. It was a poem I'd written a long time ago, and not a very good one.

There was a young man quite
                              forlorn,
Who met a quite bent leprechaun.
And he said to himself as he buggered the
                                        elf,
'I'd be far better off in an gnome.'

I nodded my head and said that, yes, it was indeed my work, and without further ado, one of my captors boomed, 'Then, sir, by order of the new republic of France and Robespierre, you are under arrest for sedition.'

It turned out that the charge against me had been trumped up. Apparently, Nina had had a miscarriage after a night out with an elk, and the public felt sorry for her. Pressure was brought to bear on the new regime, and I was to be the scapegoat . . . I'd been brought up by a billy goat. We couldn't afford a nanny.

According to the officer in charge, my poem had upset the Irish Government and they'd stopped the sale of draught Guinness and free parking in Dublin for French visitors . . . It was so obviously a frame-up, it was laughable, until, without trial, I was sent to the galleys the following day, chained to an oar, given a talk on personal hygiene, handed a bowl of hotpot with diced peacock and made to watch a performance by the crew of *Les Misérables*. The dancing was awful, but the soprano was bearable.

Day after day, in and out, we poor wretches heaved on the oars, singing old sea-shanties to the thud of the drum that marked our rhythm. Sometimes the drummer would go too fast, and the oars would smoke and the cheeks of our behinds would screech on the wooden benches and our songs turn to gibberish.

The man chained next to me was called Benny Hur. He was a big chap, and had a tattoo of someone called

Charlton Heston on his chest. We used to talk for hours on subjects ranging from the effects of turmeric on the gall bladder during a heatwave, to the possibility of blood transfusions being given to a goose laying eggs in a hat. He was a most interesting man, and champion at playing I Spy. He tried to kiss me once, but I put him off by saying I was married to a gladiator with a bad temper.

Unfortunately, the weather hadn't been very good that year, and so there weren't many people on the cruise. One or two tourists popped down to say hello and hand out sweets, but on the whole it was a quiet run. Then one morning, we heard the captain shout, 'Oh, hell. That bloody Nelson's firing at us.'

I turned to Benny Hur and asked him who this Mr Nelson was. Benny shook his mighty head. 'Nelson is England's finest seaman,' he said, 'and he's in direct competition with France for the cruise trade. He offers six days and five nights cruising round Jersey for half what we charge, and that includes afternoon tea with cucumber sandwiches or a waffle, free bingo and someone to empty your toilet bucket.'

Before I had a chance to ask any more, a cannon went off and a hole appeared in the side of our galleon. At once Benny Hur pulled out a bolt from the wall, and even as we slipped off our manacles, another round of grapeshot blew into us. Some of the galley slaves decided to write a petition to the town hall, and the others, including me, swam to freedom as the ship started to sink.

The sea was icy cold and I was damned glad I was wearing my rabbit-skin drawers, although I wished I'd killed the rabbits first. All around me was smoke from the cannons, men swimming desperately in the swollen water and attendants advertising half-price drinks during Happy Hour.

I found a spar of wood and clung to it as the battle raged. Suddenly, I was hoisted out of the sea by an English sailor . . . I knew he was English because he kept talking about the weather . . . And before I knew where I was, I was marched towards a little man with one arm and one eye.

'How are you?' he said, and gave me a kipper fillet and a pot of Earl Grey. He said he thought the weather would clear up and told me where the games room was.

Thus it came to pass that I met the great Admiral Nelson on that fateful day, and he was a real nice chap. The tourists on Nelson's ship certainly did get value for money. The cabins were a good size, with en suites and bidets. For a pound extra you could have a resident minstrel and a Chinese cold buffet on a Wednesday. There was dancing nightly and adult torture shows for anyone with a problem, plus competitive keel-haulings and Monopoly.

I was treated like a lord and I loved every minute of it, until we sailed into somewhere called Trafalgar. Nelson's mate Hardy looked a bit vexed at the sight of several French cruise ships billowing towards us, shouting through loudspeakers that they could offer a package cruise to the Orkneys, if you didn't mind being bored.

Nelson's temper snapped and he ordered his cannons to fire. Within minutes, there was total carnage, and I saw Nelson pinned to the floor with Hardy bending over him. I know full well that history states that Nelson muttered, 'Kiss me, Hardy' or even, 'Kismet, Hardy.' Well, dear reader, I was there, and I can tell you what Nelson really said. You see, before he sailed, Nelson's mistress, Mrs Hamilton, had given him some ointment for his piles, which were getting worse, owing to the sea-water finding a hole in his shorts. She didn't want the crew to see Nelson shoving the stuff up him, so she bought him a compact commode from Cairo, called a portable Karsi. Well, the last thing Nelson wanted as he lay dying was for the crew to find the Karsi and the ointment, so what he actually said to Hardy was, 'Hide my Karsi, Hardy' and with that he popped his proverbials.

After Nelson had passed on, the battle became a bit depressing, and I decided to pinch a small boat and do a bunk whilst the going was good. I didn't take much with me, just some shirts that needed ironing, a do-it-yourself appendix removal kit, a fish-embalming guide and a manual on horse-massaging in Austria. I got away with little or no trouble and set sail for Calais, but I was a bit out with my calculations and finished up in Salisbury Cathedral.

I took me a week to get the boat into the water again, and I was charged VAT for playing 'Roses of Picardy' on a trumpet during a morris dance. I felt terribly homesick, but not once did the memory of Nina enter my thoughts . . . I was well rid of the lying cow. God knows how long I spent at sea, but my beard was eight foot long and had a nest of seals in it. My lips were cracked and I longed for a glass of pure water. I was sick of drinking rare Mouton Cadet and pineapple juice.

However, Fate was on my side, for I awoke one warm morning to see the jagged shoreline of an island looming into focus. I was saved . . . or so I thought . . .

It was so wonderful to be on dry land again, I lay down and kissed the sand, failing to notice the crowd of painted savages surrounding me. It wasn't until one of them lifted me to my feet that I realized I was not alone.

A rather flatulent-looking heathen in a cheesecloth bum-cover shouted what sounded like, 'Umba muygo nahaha bugloo' and the others yelled back, 'Shamuga'. Gentle hands ferried me across the sandy shore, and every ten yards or so the natives yelled, 'Shamuga', which I took as a mark of respect . . . until I espied a huge mound of hot hippo-shit and nearly lost my balance, and the savages shouted, 'Watch out for the shamuga.'

Before long I found myself tied to a pole, placed carefully across an open fire, and it suddenly dawned on me that I was tonight's main course. Over my shoulder, I saw several naked ladies peeling onions and leeks, but just as it seemed that my fate lay in some islander's intestinal tract, a man came walking over briskly. He was dressed in a fur beret and furry shorts, and he looked a bit wild to me. By this stage I rather imagined that he'd come along for a prime cut before the others got stuck in. So his impeccable English accent came as something of a shock. 'I say there, old pagan, give the chappie some air, what? Damned bad form to eat a chap before getting to know him, old bean.' As he spoke, he flashed a wide smile of immaculate ivories, that resembled a newly white-washed fence. At once, the heathens unfastened me from the pole.

'Come with me, dear heart,' my benefactor said soothingly, and led me away. 'Sorry about the reception, old top. The trouble with these ebony bods is that they do tend to go a trifle gaga when they spot a healthy helping of protein. I say, let's go to my place and have a few drinkie-poos, what?'

My strange companion ushered me into a dormer-style mud hut with a dried moose-dung roof where, to my amazement, I saw a full-size snooker table, a rosewood cocktail trolley and a string quartet playing a selection of Lincolnshire madrigals. He saw the expression on my face and chuckled. 'Well, one is English, dear heart, and one simply must do one's best to show the jolly old flag, don't you know.'

We sipped mint juleps, served by an absolute stunner

of a native girl. The only thing she wore was a string of
beads, and three of those were sweat.

'Good heavens,' my companion said. 'Do forgive my
dashed bad manners, old hearty. Stap me if I didn't forget
to introduce myself. My name is Crusoe, Robinson
Crusoe, and this tip-top young lady, who also warms my
loins, is called Friday.' She smiled and then bowed her
way out. Crusoe refilled my glass from the carafe that
Friday had brought in, and we carried on drinking, and
I must say, Crusoe was a wonderful story-teller.

'I landed on this island about three years ago,' he said
softly. 'Before then I was at sea, serving under a most
peculiar chap called Bligh. Ever heard of him?' I shook
my head, and he carried on. 'Well, no matter. This Bligh,
well, quite frankly, he was a bit potty, and he had this
habit of exposing himself to everyone he met. We called
it flashing, and it really was dashed uncouth. There
we'd be, all ship-shape and Bristol fashion in some port
or other, the habour packed with tourists and dock
workers, then up would come Bligh in a floor-length
naval coat, and expose himself, the silly devil. Well, I
can tell you, old bean, we were the laughing-stock of the
British Fleet. He flashed everywhere and everybody.
You'd meet the old pip on the poop, and off his coat
would go and there would be his squalid little dangler
sniffing at you. One would tootle into a hotel for a gin,
and there in the corner would be Captain Bligh, coat
open, displaying his insipid little pinkie. From China to
Bombay, Iceland to Japan, Bligh flashed constantly.

'It was all getting rather horrid, and so one day, off
the coast of Borneo, a spokesman for the crew
approached me, and asked if I could talk to Bligh about
it. "After all, sir," they said, "you are a Christian
Mister." Well, this strange mode of address became my
nickname - Mr Christian - and soon that was what
everybody called me. Well, old chap, I tried speaking to

Bligh, but it was extremely difficult. He was stood on top of his desk, exposing himself, even as I spoke.

'When we landed on one of the South Sea Islands for breadfruit, Bligh walked round with his coat open, shouting loudly, "There's not many of these in a pound."'

'I tried asking him to cover himself up, but in vain. In fact, he got worse. He started asking sailors to take their trousers down and flash at people in shopping malls. This was the last straw, and the crew mutinied.

'Bligh was held down whilst somebody put his trousers back on, and then he was put on a boat with two other unfortunate sailors who had also become addicted flashers, then they were lowered into the seething ocean. The last I saw of the Captain, he was standing up in the stern of the little boat and flashing at us.'

When Crusoe finished talking, we both drank silently, each lost in his own thoughts. After a moment or so, Crusoe looked at me and grinned boyishly. 'Like to hear the rest of the story?' I nodded. I was enthralled. I hadn't enjoyed a tale so much since my Aunt Agatha had read some extracts from *The Perfumed Garden* to me. (I am a devotee of house plants.)

'After getting rid of old Bligh,' Crusoe went on, 'the rest of the voyage got a bit ghastly. There was an outbreak of sporran rash on the upper deck, and cheating at Cluedo in the bilge. The ship's formation dancing team fell out over the correct way to hold one's partner during a Polish military three-step, and Lurpak butter went up three pence a pound.' He paused as Friday glided in with a silver-plated euphonium and played, 'Nearer My God to Thee'. When she'd finished, she tap-danced on a dead banana, then cartwheeled out of the room with a mongoose up her jumper.

Crusoe and I gave her a round of applause, and then someone else bought a round and I stood up and recited one of my poems.

> The Japanese fishmonger stood in the
> dock,
> The crabs in his pants were quite
> nippy.
> When the judge cried, 'You're free,'
> He said, 'The haddock's on me,'
> And they all buggered off to the chippy.

I saw that my poem had moved my host. He asked for my autograph, then carried on with his stirring saga. 'I docked the ship at Pitcairn Island,' he said. 'Not my idea of paradise at all. Too many German tourists, for a start. Bloody Krauts, towels on the best parts of the beach and all that sort of thing. So I waved bye-bye to the crew and brought the ship here single-handedly. I didn't know how the natives would regard an intruder with a different skin colour, so the first thing I did was place an ad in the local paper, saying that I was holding a cheese and wine party, and all proceeds would go to the nearest polo team with the most home wins. Dear boy, it worked like a charm. The jolly old things cheered and walloped off the Blue Nun and red Cheddar, and we had a high time. The next day I secured a mortgage for just five anteaters and a giraffe and, as a sort of tribal blessing, the head chap threw in Friday as well as a Ewbank sweeper.'

It was clear that my new chum Robinson Crusoe had done very well for himself, and that the inhabitants of this most pleasing of islands thought the world of him. He went on to explain that the main export from the island was baked frog spit and carvings made from pickled walnuts. Apparently, the natives worshipped a god called 'Muzzelbaumittiiiooopfoy', which, roughly translated, meant 'Bert'.

The men of the tribe went about naked, apart from leather Homburgs and fishnet gloves. Twice a week, they gathered in the centre of a communal ball-bearing factory and slapped their knees with starched copies of the *Manchester Guardian* as a show of virility to the great god Bert.

The women wore simple two-piece coconut-strand skirts and peasant blouses edged with the sinews from an eel's legs and, piped along the side of the slash neck, small oysters' eyeballs nestled in a setting of burnt rubber. They spent most of their day opening offers from a mail-order catalogue and sitting by the river until the shops opened.

Generally speaking, the natives seemed healthy enough, apart from advanced syphilis of the thumb, beriberi, leprosy of the head and a total aversion to talcum powder. Amongst the young people of the island, squirrel-groping was considered the best sport by far. It was a widely held belief that a well-fondled squirrel could cure deafness in mice and stain warts on a cow's lip.

Friday was wonderful and I composed a poem about her which made my friend Crusoe very happy indeed, and he let me use his shorts.

> Dear Friday has a parrot,
> Two song birds and a kangaroo,
> And since she's been on the island,
> She's had a cockatoo.

The poem got a mention on the island's tom-tom service and I was offered a bride in exchange for a box of after-dinner mint balls.

Life was peaceful there, and I was content in the sure knowledge that the native community had accepted me. I was respected by all and sundry ... but, like most other places, there was bugger all to do on a Sundry, and I used to simply lie around or arm-wrestle with the occasional octopus that fell from a tree.

During this idyllic period, I saw very little of Robinson. He was away quite a lot on the other side of the island, looking for round-shouldered turtles to use as pith-helmet-cover stretchers. It was inevitable, I suppose, that Friday and I should seek out each other's company. I always knew where she'd be, softening buffalo hides with her teeth . . . and that's where I'd seek her . . . It was a question of hide and seek, really, which isn't a bad pun on words for an illiterate.

It thus happened on one of those steamy nights when the blood is aboil. Friday and I had been hand-rinsing some old Bibles when suddenly she leapt into my arms and shouted emotionally, 'Naw po po grr kalyy titi.' Which, I knew from my useful phrasebook, meant: 'The sandwich on my hat is coming loose under the arms.' To the more civilized of readers, that won't make much sense, but amongst the primitive tribes, it meant something quite subtle: 'I fancy a leg-over.'

Friday hurriedly undressed me with her hot hands. First she removed my Indonesian winter kilt with matching clogs, then my arm-length knee-muffs in bright burgundy, followed by my yak-hair veil and anti-corrosive semi-heated cork braces. Naked now, apart from my balsawood vest, ribbed surgical belt and sell-by-dated socks, I undressed her. Off came her canvas balaclava and Gannex ammunition belt, her chainmail cardigan and duffle scarf. Next, I divested her of a cute little leg clamp . . . it was either that or pay a fine. She took her own clay trousers off and we hit the sand entwined in each other's arms, panting with lust.

After we'd done what we wanted to do, we lay sprawled on the shore. Friday said quietly, 'Darling, do tell me, did the earth move for you?'

And it had. In fact, it was still moving. We were slap-bang in the middle of an earthquake.

The ground trembled, animals darted to and fro in terrified confusion, and billowing black smoke and cataracts of white-hot lava ejaculated from out of the huge mountain a mile away, and streamed down the slopes. I confess I was frightened, and I'd missed the football results, but Friday was a cool as could be . . . she'd locked herself in a fridge. All around us, the natives were revolting, although one or two weren't that bad, though you'd never invite them in for a hand of rummy.

Before long, the island was a turmoil of molten lava, screaming natives and double-glazing pamphlets. With my own two eyes, I saw men, women and children hurled into huge craters, and the ground closing back over them. After seeing that happen, I had a healthy respect for those gaping chasms. As far as I was concerned, it was a case of all craters great and small.

Never before had these islands known an earthquake and a volcanic eruption all in one go, and the full horror of what occurred might never be known to the outside world. Somehow, in all the panic, I'd lost Friday, but I knew that, with her experience of the Women's Institute, she'd be able to look after herself. But where was my friend Robinson Crusoe?

I made up my mind. I would go and look for him, and off I went to the other side of the island. It was a nightmare journey, but after some awesome encounters with strange life-forms calling themselves time-share reps, at last I reached the far shore, and then my heart stood still. In front of me were beach cafés, amusement arcades, a swimming lido for kids and a casino.

There weren't a lot of folk about, nor was there any evidence of the earthquake or volcanic eruption . . . It was most peculiar, and I nearly got three barrels on a fruit machine.

Suddenly, to my joy, I saw Robinson Crusoe walking along the promenade with a party of Detroit tourists who had toured the whole of Europe last Wednesday.

I felt a surge of anger. Why had he kept all this to himself? I was really vexed and decided to confront him, but I never got the chance . . . at that moment, a short, dumpy man in a long coat jumped from behind the sea groyne, shouted, 'Anyone care for a handful of this?' and opened his coat. An elderly matron from Detroit screamed, 'What's that poking out?' and her companion whispered, 'It's a penis, dear. Just like a prick, only smaller.'

I knew then that this was the Captain Bligh that my friend had talked about, and he looked like a dirty old sod.

Crusoe was furious and called for a warden to get rid of the loathsome pervert, but Bligh leapt at Crusoe, and the two men grappled like hooligans. All of a sudden, Bligh had Crusoe in a bear hug. How he managed to get out of it, I know not, but Bligh had a dreamy look on his face, and I distinctly heard him say, 'If you wrestle with it again like that I'll write you out a cheque.'

Then, without warning, the earthquake struck. Blocks of holiday flats came tumbling down . . . it was like being on the Costa Brava during Lent. The sea was so hot, fish were coming in already wrapped in newspaper.

Then my mouth went dry, for I'd just spotted Friday and Robinson in each other's arms . . . and behind them, a river of molten lava was coming closer. I cried a warning, but only a golfer with a tendency to hook heard me, and he waved me on.

It was too late, my two dear chums were surrounded, enveloped in a hiss of smoke and flame. It was a rotten way to go, but at least I had the satisfaction of knowing they were both set for life.

*

Among the debris, I managed to find a small sailing craft, and set off, away from the stricken island where I'd known such happiness, such friendship. Dear Robinson. I would never forget him, nor indeed, the lovely Friday. But soon I had to stop my sad musings, for a storm was blowing up and a bad one it was ... Mountainous waves crashed and fell on my frail vessel and an incensed wind whipped the sea to even greater fury. That was on Monday. On Tuesday, the sky grew black and forked fire speared the ocean that lashed my aching body. The wind howled like a lost soul in torment, and the bitter, cold force of the sea pounded my ship into matchsticks. Wednesday was half-day closing. I tumbled out of my wrecked craft and battled to stay afloat, although I knew the Grim Reaper was holding out his hand to me. Up and down, from side to side, the elements tossed me. My lungs strove for air as vast sheets of water cascaded over my head. I felt life slipping away slowly from my numbed body and mind ... My life seemd to travel along before my eyes ... Odd little incidents came to life in front of me ...

I was six years old and Daddy was trying to teach me to swim in the canal. 'Don't throw me over the side again, Daddy,' I could hear myself saying. I didn't mind him wanting to make me swim, but for a wee chap of only six summers, escaping from the sack each time was a bugger ... Now I was sixteen, dressed in velvet doublet and hose with a plumed hat, and carrying a nosegay of violets for my new-found love, Alicia. She was adorable, breathtakingly fresh and a dead cert. Her father was so rich, when they held a fox hunt, the fox had to show references before they'd agree to chase it ... Now, the death of my grandmother presented its forlorn image to my drowning senses ... Nobody was sorry to see her pop off. My father couldn't wait to have her buried. In fact, he took the corpse to the graveyard

on the back of a Derby winner. But I had a strange
feeling Grandma wasn't really dead. When we threw
soil on the coffin, she started throwing it back . . . Then
I saw myself at school, answering all the teacher's
questions on algebra. How strange, is it not? I was
excellent at algebra at school, and now I don't speak a
word of it . . . As my past life zoomed in front of me, one
thought stood out: up to now I'd been a real boring fart.

I felt myself sliding into damp oblivion. My arms were
leaden and my lower limbs and torso were numb. My
lungs cramped, and as if all that wasn't enough to
torment a man, I desperately needed to go to the
lavatory. Death was beginning to throw his cape over
me. I felt blissfully uncaring about life and, indeed, I
was laughing madly and winking at a school of turbot.

I hardly remember the hands that grabbed my sodden
body. All I can dimly recall is a well-modulated voice
saying above the roar of the sea, 'Has he any money on
him?'

I'm told I slept for a week and, by the Lord Harry, I
was nursed back to health by a middle-aged sailor who
had been struck off the National Health register after
treating the Duke of Wellington for influenza of the foot.
He was bitter about the incident, particularly about
getting the boot from Wellington.

Soon, however, I was up and about, clambering on to
the deck of the ship, and what a fine ship it was. The
crew were immaculately dressed in roguish shorts and
cotton polo-necked jumpers, with trilbies perched on top
of their pigtailed bobs. The captain, a dandy by the
name of Beau Brummel, was exquisitely clothed. He
wore a high-neck satin halter atop his silk Malay-style
shirt. His long, pulled-in-at-the-waist hacking jacket in
autumn brown would have been the talk of any hunt
meet, and his superbly cut cavalry twill trousers, and
shining high leather boots with gold spurs, were

perfection. To complete the ensemble, a heavy gold Italian carved quizzing-glass hung on a velvet ribbon round his neck. As for his wide-brimmed hat adorned with osprey feathers, it was sheer delight.

Beau Brummel's was a strange story . . . Apparently, he'd been a great friend of an English prince, but they'd fallen out over the colour of a waistcoat and he'd been given the push from Court society. For a time he had sold made-to-measure cuff-links for orphans on a pension, but one night a thug set fire to his tray. Of course, he'd applied for a rent rebate and a new appliance from the rupture clinic, but then his wife tried to bite a Grand National winner, and his library ticket was revoked.

At his wits' end, which I'd always thought was a silly name for a house, he decided to get away from it all, to be isolated, alone in the wilderness, so he went to live in Lowestoft. He did some male modelling for a fashion house and then opened a chip shop, which didn't do well because the casino kept complaining about the hot fat on the roulette table. (I know that doesn't make much sense, but it seemed funny at the time, which proves what lack of decent food can do.) Then one night, a seafaring man who couldn't pay the fare had his ship confiscated, and Brummel bought it as a sort of floating male boutique. From the start it was a howling success . . . and so Brummel renamed the ship after a lady he'd once dallied with in an ostler's overcoat, the *Marie Celeste*.

I quickly made myself useful, by doing the sewing and ironing each day before we docked and the wholesalers came on board, Although I say it myself, my needlework was excellent, and nobody could iron a frogged lapel like yours truly. We did very well in Liverpool and Wigan with Brummel's hand-painted clogs and flared scarves, but Runcorn was bloody awful . . . still is.

Next, we sailed to the land of the Norsemen, but all they wanted were axes, dead skins for jock-straps and invitations to a rape detail. Holland was much better, and Brummel's new fashion of Afro-Hungarian sleeveless pullovers with built-in anti-mugging devices inside a clown's briefcase which hung from a puce shoulder-strap to a peg, rawl-plugged into the eardrum, were the hit of the show. From Rotterdam we sailed to France, where our garlic-impregnated berets had the Parisians lining the streets. Soon the money was rolling in and Beau Brummel was seriously thinking of extending the ship and putting a cafeteria in the bilge.

The trouble started in Brest, if my mammary serves me right, and that is a dreadful pun. Always on the lookout for new ways to promote his creations, Brummel announced that the theme for his next show was going to be magic.

This announcement did not come as any great surprise to the crew. In the past, Beau Brummel had utilized show-girls and jesters to promote his range of men's clothing, and on one occasion he had employed Sumo wrestlers to model Tyrolean underwear for the larger man.

This time Brummel went straight to the top, and hired one of Euorpe's greatest illusionists, whose 'Giraffe in a Rissole' is still the talk of the Magic Circle wherever they may gather. Fantastic Roberto was enough to draw the biggest crowds, and there was some suggestion of a week in Blackpool.

As soon as the news got about, tickets to see Brummel's fashion show with a special appearance by Roberto sold like hot griddle cakes. As the big night approached, the atmosphere of excitement was almost tangible, and we had to rent half a dozen portaloos.

From the moment I met Roberto I was impressed. He stood six foot three whatever the weather, and possessed piercing eyes and a fine Roman nose, which stood in the middle. The entire crew were mesmerized by his tricks. He produced an iron banana from the bosun's wooden leg and then bounced it across a bucketful of fudge. He impressed all of us on board the good ship *Marie Celeste*, but none more than Beau Brummel himself . . . He couldn't take his eyes off the magician. Roberto's main illusion for the floating fashion show was his celebrated Disappearing Cabinet. The idea was that, on the night, all the male models would parade one by one down the catwalk, twirl, then retrace their steps back to the cabinet. Roberto would then draw a curtain across the front, and, after a second's pause, draw it back again and, hey presto! the models would vanish. The illusion would be repeated until all that remained was the audience.

Things were going well, and we sold a gross of hand-painted underpants with sea-repellent cotton buds sewn in the waistband. But one thing bothered me: Beau Brummel's preoccupation with the magician and his skill. Roberto's Disappearing Cabinet had him transfixed . . . and when I looked deep into Brummel's burning stare, I sensed madness of the brain.

We set sail from Brest with over five thousand francs in a tin chest and a captain who'd gone silly over magic tricks. He got on the crew's nerves with his incessant pulling an egg out of someone's ear trick. It drove one sailor to drown himself in a keg of ship's rum . . . awful death, took six hours to die. Mind you, he got out of the barrel eight times to visit the gents'.

Things came to a head, including a boil on my neck, one hot and extremely calm day. The day watch had just danced the Gay Gordons for a charity cross-country runner who'd had his hip off when I heard moaning coming from inside a small bag of cold cheese. Imagine my consternation when I opened the bag and discovered the splendidly dressed figure of Roberto the magician.

'Good grief,' I stammered. 'I thought you'd got off the ship in Brest.'

Roberto grabbed my arm tightly. 'I was kidnapped by Brummel,' he said hoarsely. 'He said if I didn't teach him how to do the Disappearing Cabinet illusion, he'd tell Equity that the doves up my back are rubber. I had to obey . . . the doves *are* made of rubber. Live ones suffocate in my dinner-jacket sleeve because of my BO.'

This was serious and no mistake, me hearties, for his BO was indeed stomach-turning. In fact, in comparison, when he broke wind it was like the smell of spring flowers in a window-box.

A chill ran down my back when it dawned on me suddenly that some of the crew seemed to be missing. Roberto noticed it as well and we looked at each other and paled, for we both knew what was happening . . .

Silently we crept down into the very heart of the ship, to see that our suspicions were correct. Beau Brummel was making the crew disappear.

'Stop this madness!' Roberto and I shouted in unison, but Brummel simply grinned wolfishly and carried on pushing the men into the cabinet. At some signal, which neither Roberto nor I saw, two burly sailors grabbed us by the arms and in a trice, we were both tied up.

Soon the insane captain had done it . . . all the crew had disappeared, and only the three of us were left on the *Marie Celeste*. My plight gave me added strength and I found that my bonds were coming loose. I twisted my wrists and felt the knots stretching. Meanwhile, with foam round his lips, the imbecile captain, once an intellectual dandy with extended credit at Barclays, was dragging Roberto towards the infernal cabinet. In vain, the magician struggled to take a final bow, and as he was trundled through the curtain he just managed to shout, 'Cancel my digs in Crewe.'

The captain threw back his head, gave an ear-splitting shriek of triumph, and walked over to me. I pretended to be still trussed up and, as he bent over me, I sprang. Holding him by the shoulders, I brought my knees up to my chest, then pushed. The potty captain performed a parabola and skidded into the cabinet and oblivion . . . I was alone on the *Marie Celeste*.

It was quite nice at first, but the novelty palled after I'd played deck quoits and had a dip in the pool. I don't remember how long I was at sea but I was having a catnap when I heard someone coming aboard. Footsteps rang down the gangway towards my cabin and, not knowing if they belonged to pirates or Customs and Excise, which are more or less the same thing, I hid behind the door. When it opened, a hairy, rather ghastly-looking sailor peeped in, and when he saw that the cabin was vacant, he backed out again. I tiptoed out after him and became part of the boarding party. Not a soul questioned my presence.

I had a funny feeling that the *Marie Celeste* would be a big point of discussion amongst seafaring men, but I never imagined that the story of the crewless ship would become the greatest mystery of the sea. Many a time I was tempted to relate the truth of what really happened, but let's face it, who would have believed me?

The first thing I did on coming ashore was to join Napoleon's army as a landscape gardener, although there didn't seem to be much call for one after the cock-up at Moscow, and so they promoted me to Napoleon's batman, with a rise in pay and a choice of free-range eggs. From the start it was obvious that Napoleon was a poof. His boyfriend, an ex-Austrian clog-dancer called Josef, was never away from Boney's tent, and I never had enough room to do my ironing. Napoleon also had a woman who fancied him, but he couldn't be bothered, and once when she called round, he said firmly, 'Not tonight, Josef's in.'

After Elba, I decided to desert the army because I was
fed up, and the sand irritated my piles. Napoleon was
muttering on about having another crack at raising an
army, but the Elba Tourist Board wouldn't give him any
time off and then Josef ran off with a glue salesman.

My spell of liberty was brief. Before long, I was picked
up by the military police at a cheese and wine party in a
Hall of Mirrors Fun House, and taken to Paris, where
retribution was swift.

To my horror, I was sent to the dreaded Château d'If
for three months. My soul screamed with torment as I
lay in that black stinking hole. For over a week I lay
there, holding my nose, until the jailer pointed out that I
was lying at the bottom of a very large sanitary bucket.
From that day on, things got better, although the
Nubian nymphomaniacs tended to slop their wine jars
on orgy nights, making the tiles round the Jacuzzi a bit
slippery. Generally, though, everything was hunky-
dory, and I was looking forward to a week in Tenerife
when some new prisoners arrived and started talking
about escaping. This worried me a lot.

Fortunately, my sentence came to an end before
anybody got idiotic enough to attempt an escape. Once
free, I went to Paris for a short holiday, and relaxed in
the arms of a nice lady who did incredible things with a
bottle and a Turk's lance, and I read a lot of back copies
of *Good Housekeeping.*

One night, after a pleasant evening with the lady's
lance and a mixed grill, I dozed off on her clothes-rack,
only to be roughly awakened by the most grotesque
human being I have ever seen. She had the skin of a
freshly boiled hippo in labour. Her hair, what was left of
it, had been dyed so often she had technicolour
dandruff, and she was so bowlegged, she must have had
to iron her drawers on a boomerang. Her nose was so

flat she had to cover her ears with a hankie to blow it, and her eyes were so crossed, if they watered, the tears ran down her back. Her three teeth stuck out so far, she could chew an apple through a tennis racquet and she had so many warts on her chins, she had to wash with Braille soap. The muscles on her neck and shoulders rippled through the mat of black hair that grew in wild profusion on her upper torso, and her breasts were so enormous she couldn't wear a bra, she had to use baling wire. The good lady's arms were the width and

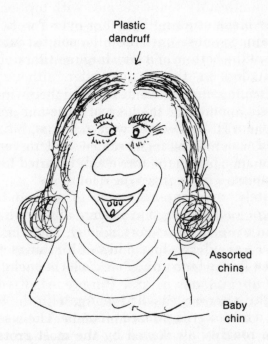

Plastic
dandruff

Assorted
chins

Baby
chin

BUST OF FLORENCE THE WHORE!

Made at a safe distance by a German cow's-udder
specialist inside a clown's trousers whilst looking
for a spanner. Apricots were two pence cheaper in
Bacup, my mum told me.

thickness of an average bull's waist, and she told me that her name was Florence and that she was expecting a child. The father was a man called Pierre Le Toq, and she had reason to believe that I had met him in the Château d'If . . .

After she lifted me off the floor with one ham-sized fist and banged my head repeatedly against her knee, I casually mentioned that I had indeed met the gentleman in question. She grunted with satisfaction and impaled me on the coat-stand before lumbering off, presumably to pack her belongings in readiness to leave for the Château.

I wasted no time. I wasn't that fond of Le Toq, but if he had put the bun in that harlot's oven, at least he deserved a chance to attend an out-patients'. I wriggled off the hook and crept away.

The following day, I went to the job centre and successfully applied for the post of assistant jailer at the Château d'If. The wages were nominal, but there was a pension-cum-investment scheme and free parking for pensioners. Here is the torrid tale of how I became involved once again in this historical romp . . .

When I informed Le Toq that Florence knew where he was, the poor man howled like a dervish, so Robin Hood heated up some chicken soup and sold him a watch. Big Wally, with Quasimodo up his back, was bouncing a set of twins up and down, and Pimply Al, Fred and Edmond Dantés sang, 'We'll Meet Again'.

At once, plans were laid for an escape. The best idea came from, of all people, Walter the Moron. His plan was simplicity itself: the Château was on an island, right? Well, all they had to do was detach the island from the seabed, then they could sail away. Everybody was so excited by this that they gave Walter a leather banana to screw to his sleeve, and we all had a vindaloo.

As time passed, we all worked to smuggle things into the jail that would help us escape – little things like steam hammers and dynamite, shire horses to lug the rock away, Irish navvies and an accordion band. It wasn't always smooth sailing, though. No, by the blood of Odin, it wasn't, but after a month, the island was free, and, using one of Wally's shirts, we floated out to sea on a stiff wind that carried on it the good wishes of a water diviner who was having trouble with his foot. We used Walter's head as a compass and travelled east in a westerly direction but on a northern tack that led us south past Wally's earhole. It was to be the start of a truly great and stupid adventure, and I am proud to have been part of it.

READERS' JOKE COMPETITION

Why did the chicken, knowing full well that it was perverted, decide to cross the road on a Thursday of all days? . . . Because it was in a foul mood and it's too busy on Friday.

(The above excellent joke was sent in by a lapsed crooner with the Co-op meat department. In his letter to us, he states that he is fond of hiding mice in a grapefruit during a crisis. He lives under his mother, but says that she's getting a bit heavy since she painted the Blitz, and he longs for a loudspeaker, if only to sit in. His Name is Fogal Blueberry and his head gets hot if he bends down in cement. He is fond of his feet and wishes one of them had a sister.)

AND NOW . . . THE STORY CONTINUES . . .

A FEW WORDS FROM
SIR WALTER RALEIGH'S DIARY

I'd just about had enough, I can tell you. Months spent in the New World dodging bloody arrows and living off hot dogs had utterly depressed me and the lads, and no mistake. To begin with, those Red Indians have no sense of humour. I said to one of them: 'What tribe are you from?' He was a big fellow with nothing on and what I saw depressed me even more. 'Me, Blackfoot,' he said. I smiled and replied, 'Yes, and your neck's a funny colour as well.' Not a bad gag, worth a chuckle. From him, nothing.

I tried again. 'Me make hot poultices for bald Indians.' He just looked at me, then he said, 'I don't give a shit.'

'No, no,' I shouted. 'Me make hot poultices for bald Indians ... They keep their wigs-warm ... Get it? Wigwams.' The bronzed sod never turned a hair, just waddled off to a Bring and Buy scalp stall.

I was having it away with a Crow ... nice bird but raven mad ... Ha, ha, ha, get it? God's beard! Life was boring. Fights were breaking out at the tombola and the more sex-starved members of the ship's company were breaking off engagements with turkeys, after finding it difficult to pee with fowl pest.

I shudder to think what would have happened if we hadn't stumbled across an Indian chip shop. For days we'd been buying up loads of a weed called tobacco, merely because a sailor heard a Jesuit missionary say that smoking it gave you an erection. I tried it a few times, and it wasn't that bad if you rolled it up tightly – the tobacco, I mean.

Well, anyway, we were all marching back to the ship, playing I Spy to while away the journey, when one of the lads said, 'There's a grand smell coming from yonder.'

We took a peep and saw this glass-fronted shop . . . the Indian behind the counter said, 'Me have cod and hake left, but no mushy peas. You will have to wait for chips because the fat needs changing.'

We all knew what cod and hake was, of course, but none of us knew what chips were. 'What are chips?' I asked politely. The Indian wiped his brow and turned the steam down on the steak puddings. 'Chips come from potato,' he said. Well, as you can imagine, once the crew had sampled chips there was no holding them, and the Indian kept putting the prices up. And so it was that I started growing potatoes myself, and selling them to the crew a groat cheaper than the Indian chippy.

He retaliated by giving away a packet of crisps with every double bag of chips sold, which forced me to undercut his faggots and black peas by nearly 15 per cent a plate. He came right back into the price war with table service and free beer, the bastard.

Well, I got even by introducing my own waiter service and orchestra plus a speciality act to amuse the customers. The Indian then opened another shop, a two-storey building, waiter service upstairs and self-service downstairs. I went into partnership with the ship's carpenter, a hearty man called Wimpy, and introduced steak and chips to the lads and we did a burster. Soon I was getting all the Apache business, and even the 7th Cavalry started queuing up with Custer for hamburger take-aways. I didn't half miss him when he messed up at Little Big Horn.

I know, I know, I should have stayed in America, but Queen Elizabeth sent word that she was fed up waiting for me to bring some treasure home, and if something didn't happen soon she'd stuff my head with kapok and play the World Cup with it. I had no choice, really, so I sold the business to a trader, a man called McDonald, and sailed back to England and my sovereign. Queen Liz was blazing mad about the length of time I'd been away, and was considering sending me to the Tower. So I wasted no time in booking a coach to London. In my pockets I carried my two discoveries . . . tobacco and a potato. They would be my salvation, I hoped.

The Court, as usual, was full of spies, gossips, whores and liberals who'd lost their deposits. The Queen sat on the spare throne . . . the other one was away being varnished. Her face was about as pleasant to look at as a dead cow in an open grave.

'Come here bugger-lugs,' she hissed. I bowed and knelt before her. 'Come on, Walter,' she said sharply. 'What have you brought me?'

I got to my feet, my face flushed with pride, and, keeping my eyes lowered, took one of my surprises out of my pocket. 'Pray place this between your lips, my Queen,' I boomed to the whole court. 'Have you done so?' I went on. Liz grunted, and I sparked my flint into fire (I'd left my Ronson on the mantelpiece), igniting the object in her most royal of gobs.

I expected her to whoop with joy and give me a few bob, but to my horror, she coughed, spat and grated, 'What the bleedin' hell do you call this?'

I couldn't believe it when I looked. 'It's called a potato,' I said.

They had me in the Tower before I could say a thing, and I knew that my fate was sealed. I'd be asked to join the Masons after my *faux pas*, either that or my bus-pass would be taken off me.

The days rolled into weeks and I gave up all hope of
getting out of the Bloody Tower. And then Fate stepped
into my life, in the shape of Mary, Queen of Scots. She
was in the next-door cell, but that presented no problem,
because, as in every historical tale, I'd found a secret
passage in my shorts which led directly to it. Within a
week, or it could have been less because I'm not very
good at geography, Mary and I were smoking pot and
doing naughty things in the straw. She was damn good
company and a fine harpist . . . pity we didn't have one.
When I told her what had happened over the potato
incident, she laughed merrily. She must have seen the
look on my face for she whispered, 'Fear not, Walter. I
have a master plan for an escape and a bag of biscuits as
a raffle prize.' Swiftly she outlined her plan . . .

Two of her ladies-in-waiting were coming to see her
for morning coffee on Thursday. Her plan was for us to
hypnotize them into thinking they were us! We would
then walk out disguised as the two ladies-in-waiting,
and try to find out what they were waiting for.

It worked a treat. As soon as the two elegant women
arrived, with a packet of Bath Olivers and a copy of
Woman's Realm, I slipped into Mary's cell. I told them a
joke about Queen Elizabeth and a kangaroo, and as
they tittered I gently swung a bright bauble to and fro.

'You are no longer you, for you are I and I am you,' I
intoned. One lady's eyes glazed over. I turned to her
companion. 'You are no longer you, for you are she and
she is you.' They were now both under the influence and
we had to work fast. Mary stripped one woman and I
stripped the other. By the left she were bonnie and no
mistake. Her arse was pink and dimpled . . . ooooohhh!

'Come on, pull yourself together, you dirty sod,' Queen
Mary whispered. 'What are you doing with that pig?' It
was indeed true, I realized, peering into the gloom. I'd
been undressing a pig.

Finally the deed was done, and Mary and I walked casually out of the dungeon dressed as the two ladies-in-waiting, leaving the Tower behind us. We were free! On impulse, I turned round, and saw the pig beckoning me back.

I don't know what happened to Mary after that, but I heard she'd opened a wine-bar in North Camden and owned a fighting cock. For myself, I signed on as an ordinary seaman aboard a merchant vessel, bound for the Indies with a cargo of molasses and council-house wallpaper. It was a rotten journey and I was sick three times after eating sticky buns. The crew were awful . . . one of them was so dirty, after he'd had a bath, you had to poke the water down the plug-hole with a stick. I didn't like the captain either. He only had one leg, and he kept calling me, 'Jim, Lad' and his parrot smelt.

We had been at sea for a fortnight when the lookout spotted an island on the horizon. In vain, the captain and I scoured our maps with aching eyeballs, but there was no island charted in this part of the ocean. Yet there it was, getting closer. Of course, the crew claimed it was a ghost ship and a retired solicitor jumped overboard. I must admit, it did seem rather peculiar, and just as I had warned the captain to arm the men, the island bumped into us.

'Hello,' came a voice from the island. 'Are we anywhere near Bolton?'

'Who speaks?' croaked our worthy captain.

'My name is Pierre Le Toq and my companions and I are at present in the Château d'If.' Our faces were a picture, and so we starting selling tickets. However, it was true. Pierre and his brave band of intrepid adventurers had indeed uprooted the island from the seabed and sailed it across the ocean.

We all crowded around Quasimodo, for the little man was a big favourite in England, and Shakespeare was

going to write a play about him. I especially liked the
poetry of Louis Bovary. Even after all these years, I
cannot forget one haunting ode that he composed
during a beetle-drive:

> The boy stood on the burning deck,
> He was eating chips and scallops.
> A burning piece of mast fell
> down his chest and incinerated
> His bollocks.

Without regret, I left the merchant ship and joined the
strange crew on the island . . . and a strange lot they
were too. Walter the Moron – well, if brains had been
skin, that idiot wouldn't have had enough for a flea's
foreskin! As for the enigmatic Pimply Al, he spent most
of his time drawing faces round his spots, and little
Quasimodo did nothing but practise his swordsmanship
and send fan-mail to Snow White.

Our navigation was somewhat erratic, but we finally
landed the island in North Wales. The weather was
atrocious; it rained incessantly. I said to one Welshman
who was singing to a leek, 'We're getting pissed on.'

'You're lucky, boyo,' he replied. 'Last week I got
snowed on.'

At this, I looked meaningfully at my companions, and
there and then, we decided to call the Château d'If
'Snowdon'.

We didn't stay in Wales for long, however. The pubs
were shut and Walter the Moron couldn't bounce
anybody because they all seemed to wear long pointed
hats which pricked his palms. In any case, Robin Hood
was anxious to get back to his shop in Sherwood. Maid
Marian had to get ready for the sales, and the
wholesalers couldn't say when the frocks she'd ordered

would be delivered. This year, Marian was going for the Nottingham Look . . . slash neck, peasant hem with a lace flounce, puff sleeves trimmed in organdie strips and a clay tulip on an arm-band.

Since the nights were drawing in, I suggested that we all climbed up on to Walter's back and accompanied Robin to Nottingham.

It was a bit of a squeeze, I must say, but we found a branch of High and Mighty in Rhyl and we bought Walter an enormous waterproof latex sheet. After fitting it with bunk beds and stirrups, we all managed to get some rest while the giant trudged across the mountains, bouncing a female Druid we'd captured earlier in the day.

In future times it's possible that people will turn to each other in bus queues and say blithely, 'What was old Walter Raleigh famous for?'

Well, it won't be for discovering bloody fags, I can tell you. But it would be rather nice if, in years to come, the country was awash with 'Fish and Raleigh Chip Shops' . . . and why not? After all, it was I that saw the best potential for the common spud.

These were the thoughts that crossed my mind as I tried to snatch a brief kip up big Walter the Moron's cardigan. What a nightmare! He smelt like an Arabian culvert, and I'd lost most of my clothes playing strip-dominoes inside his vest.

I couldn't stand it any more. I simply had to get away from my odd companions. One night, as Walter was climbing through the Welsh mountains, I slid down his braces while the others finished off their square dance, and ran as swiftly as possible towards a tiny village nestling between two towering peaks. It was much further than I had thought and soon I was knackered.

I had just decided to cover myself with bracken and pretend I was asleep in a Holiday Inn when a man approached me, wearing a large hat and riding a big black horse waving a gun. I'd never seen a horse wave a gun before, except when I'd had a drink . . .

'Stand and deliver,' the man said.

'Deliver what?' I asked.

He wagged a long finger at me. 'You heard, mush . . . Stand and deliver.'

I scratched my head, which happened to be the nearest thing. There were other things which I yearned passionately to scratch, but this is a book for the whole family, not for some dirtly little Soho-haunting git. 'I'd like to help you, sir,' I said politely. 'But I don't know what you want me to deliver.'

The man got off his horse and asked me to hold his pistol whilst he pulled a jigsaw puzzle from under his hat. 'I'm not sure, old bean,' he said gently. 'But old habits die hard, don't you know, and before I became a highwayman I worked in the post office.'

His name was Dick Turnip. He was a Swede, but knew his onions and was full of beans. At the post office he'd had a regular celery and now lettuce hope that these pathetic puns will cease, if only to peas me . . .

Dick was good company, but suddenly he told me something that made my blood run cold. He mentioned a name that stirred a chord in my memory . . . the name was Florence, the Whore of Paris. Rumours of her ugliness had reached my ears, even in the New World. More frightening had been the story that Attila the Hun was her bastard child. Yes, dear, outraged reader . . . Attila the Hun was a chap with so many problems, not even Claire Rayner could have helped him.

As I listened, a thought full of foreboding flashed across my mind . . . my strange companions had spoken of Pierre le Toq once having had a leg-over with Flo. And hadn't I heard that Florence was expecting another little bastard? All of a sudden, I remembered

the ancient curse recently popularized by spittoon
thieves:

> There was an old maid from Genoa,
> And I blush when I think what I owe her.
> Now she's gone to her rest,
> And it's all for the best,
> Otherwise I'd have to borrow Somoa.

It was getting late now, and Turnip looked beet, and I
was bursting for a leek myself. As a measure of
friendship, I gave Turnip my ring, which was nine
carrot. He was so moved, his face went a radish colour,
and he said, 'I yam moved.' I thought, Hi, hi, mate,
that's shallot. Frankly, I couldn't wait for the marrow to
come.

In the morning Turnip cantered away to the city of
York, and I realized that I had to find my friends, and
tell them what I knew about Florence. The future of
England, nay, the world and possibly even Gateshead
West might be threatened by another of her bastards.

As I watched Turnip fall off his horse in the distance, I
saw the purpling hills capture the blush of the evening
sun as it rested its warmth along the crest of the horizon,
and the tints caught the rolling meadows in a sprawl of
colour that threw violet glances at a mirror of water that
lay dappled by a yawning black void of forest deep. And
somewhere behind a cow-shed a car was sick.

Everybody was glad to see me again, and Quasimodo
returned the galoshes and comic apron he'd won off me
at strip-dominoes. When I told my gallant companions
what I'd heard, they were aghast and so was I, but I put
it down to the baked beans.

We set off for Nottingham, to take the pressure off
Robin Hood, who was worried about Maid Marian's
attitude. The Man in the Iron Mask was feeling so lost

without the mask that Edmond Dantés welded his head into a billy can.

The weather was appalling. It rained so much, they were having lifeboat drill in hotel bedrooms. Three times, Quasimodo had to jump from under Walter's pullover to fight off English soldiers who challenged our little party. The dwarf certainly could fence . . . he did an entire garden in under an hour. As for Walter, he nearly got us arrested when he bounced a fat beefeater against a lamp-post, and the entire village chased us with time-share offers. We heard disturbing news that Bonnie Prince Charlie was stuck in Preston without a change of laundry . . . someone had certainly got wind of that.

At last, a month later, we arrived on the outskirts of Nottingham, and spent the night at an inn before setting forth into the forest. What lay before us? I knew not. All I was aware of was that we were living in momentous days, but the nights were a bit dull and there wasn't a striptease show in town.

READERS' JOKE COMPETITION

In a democratic society a perverted chicken has every right to cross a road on a Thursday. The problem here is why cross the road at all? . . . Obviously because to do something naughty with another bent chicken he has to cross the road to get at it!

(Submitted by Miss Wallis Ballpoint from Bradford East. This is a thought-provoking joke which was very popular in small parcels during a singsong in a welfare lighthouse. Miss Ballpoint wallpapers children for money and has never watched Brookside *through the base of a jug. Her brother holds the record for stapling fish to a rentbook under warm Marmite. He lives up a tree now.)*

RIGHT . . . NOW THERE'S MORE OF THE BOOK
TO THRILL YOU . . .

MAID MARIAN

I should have listened to my mother. Right from the start, she warned me that Robin Hood was a basket case. Frankly, I'd go even further – he's a waste of skin.

What I ever saw in that crack-pot I'll never know. But I was young at the time, fed up living in a draughty castle with bad plumbing, and the curtains – well, I tell you, I'd have run up a few sets myself, but my guardian, the Sheriff of Nottingham, wouldn't hear of the expense. What got my goat was that I could have bought a sample roll of velvet from a man I know at the market.

I suppose what attracted me to wandering about the forest was the thought of getting away from all the parties my guardian kept throwing for that awful Prince John. I'd never met the true King, Richard the Lionheart, but apparently he was as gay as a second-hand goose, with a penchant for young morris dancers and flute players. On more than one occasion, I heard my guardian say that he'd like to shove a pikestaff up the King's arse, but that he'd probably only ask for a pike with a longer handle.

Like many girls, I had to watch my weight, what with all the food at these feasts – chicken, suckling pig, braised peacock with thyme, boar's brains in brandy sauce, half a roasted calf with new potatoes and placed on a bed of hot horse livers, lightly grilled turtle's ankles

101

in a curry dip with individually sewn whitebait . . . and those were just the starters! As you can imagine, I couldn't get into many of my C & A frocks after a week of that lot. The peasants didn't realize how lucky they were to be living on a diet of bread and dripping. I could never understand why so many of them were dead.

At any rate, I felt fat and unwanted. The castle minstrels kept playing the top ten madrigals over and over again, and it was giving me a headache, so I took myself off to the forest. I could walk a few pounds off and have the odd puff on a Woodbine.

Most days the forest was deserted, apart from a few Japanese tourists and the odd sexual deviant, but on this particular morning, I noticed fresh horse-manure, and then I saw the body of a soldier holding his nose. At once I was alarmed . . . it's a neat alarm, just one wire leading from my hip to a crotch battery . . . Of course, I'd heard of the outlaws who lived in Sherwood, of how they would rape and pillage innocent women, but try as I might, I couldn't see a single outlaw anywhere.

Suddenly, I heard a rustling in the undergrowth, and a man in green tights jumped out in front of me.

'What have we got here?' he boomed. 'A defenceless maid in the forest deep? Robin must know of this. Come, girl.' And with that, he tucked me under one arm and we went crashing through the undergrowth.

He told me that his name was Little John, which was a silly name for such a big, fine-looking man. I wondered idly if he was on rape detail and made a mental note to find out, and put myself down on his list of victims.

The journey seemed to take an eternity. The bones in my corset had almost bent into a circle, and I would have killed for a cup of tea.

Eventually we reached a large clearing. Huts made of branches encircled the area, and there was a big sort of community fire in the middle, with an ox roasting over it. Then I noticed a long, low, double-fronted shop with ladies' clothes hanging in the window. There was a sale on, and there was a lovely two-piece bolero-style skirt and jacket, with a wisp of a chiffon scarf to offset the saucy wide-brimmed Fedora. In Nottingham, the price of an outfit like that would have been more than a woodcutter earned in ten years. The name over the shop door read: 'Robinsky. Master Bespoke Tailor for Ladies of Quality'.

Little John put me down outside the shop and shouted, 'Robin! Come and see what I found in the forest deep.'

Back came the reply: 'You want that I should drop a stitch already, you schmuck?'

Little John grinned. 'I have a lady here, and she looks as though she could be a good customer.'

That did the trick, and a middle-sized thin man wearing green tights and a T-shirt bounded out of the shop with a smile that stretched from ear to ear. 'Charmed, I'm sure, my lady. You want that I should show you the latest lines from gay Paree?' Then he kissed my hand . . . his lips felt like a burst Cumberland sausage.

That was my first meeting with Mendel Robinsky, now known as Robin Hood. I bought the outfit in the window and he gave me a good discount for paying with unmarked gold bars, and threw in two pairs of double-gusseted bloomers as well.

Looking back, I think the tailor won his way to my heart with flattery, generous discounts and chicken soup. For the life of me, I couldn't picture him as an outlaw. For while his Merry Men carried bows and arrows, he held a tape-measure and chalk. In the middle of one pitched battle with Prince John's men, Robin took seven orders for open-necked jerkins and three-quarter plus-fours.

I'd like to say a word or two about the so-called 'Merry Men's here. The truth is, they were the most miserable old sods I've ever seen. Moan, moan, bloody moan, that's all they did from morn till dusk. If it wasn't the weather, it was the price of arrows, or the shortage of good toilet paper. Friar Tuck was one of the most discontented people I have ever met. He was so fat that for a number of years he worked as a decoy for a whaling fleet. He had so many chins, I always had the impression he was resting his head on a pile of crumpets. And I've never seen anyone eat as much as that old fake. One night he had six bread rolls with butter, two braised geese, a full salmon and a Wimpy double cheeseburger with relish. When Will Scarlett asked, 'What would you like to wash it down with?' somebody said, 'Try Lake Windermere.'

That's not all . . . Allen a-Dale sang out of tune, and he made up some pretty rude songs about me:

> Maid Marian tends her veg patch
> In Sherwood 'neath the trees,
> And when she feels a little tired
> She sits among the cabbages and peas.

That one used to infuriate me, but the one that really made me blow my top was this dirty ditty:

> Robin and his Merry Men,
> They frolic in the sun.
> If you ask, 'Who's Maid Marian?'
> The men say, 'Everyone.'

Well! At the time, Robin hadn't even laid so much as a finger on me – not that I was all that bothered. He wasn't exactly a sex symbol, and I've had more fun with a length of cucumber. For a start his nose was so big, it kept the sun off his face. He was so skinny, he had to part his hair in the middle, in case he overbalanced. In fact, he was so thin, if he swallowed tomato juice he looked like a thermometer. Quite frankly, if he'd had another navel, he'd have been a flute. But I suppose that living in the forest deep made me feel romantic, and so I took him home to meet Mother.

As soon as she set eyes on him, she mouthed, 'Prat' to me. Still, she made a rabbit casserole and we all had a glass of sherry while Robin explained why he lived with his friends in Sherwood.

'My life has been full of tragedy,' he said quietly. 'My parents owned a council house in Stoke, but one day the town hall said that because we were so far behind with the rent, they were holding my father hostage. This news sent my mother a trifle peculiar and she began to think she was a hen. Oh, I wanted to take her to see a doctor, but we needed the eggs at the time. Then one night she fell asleep on a waterbed and was poached to death.

'We were so poor we hardly had enough gold to bury dear Mother. My father bought a pinewood coffin, but when my eldest sister saw it (she was home on leave from a Polish artillery piano band), she said angrily, "Pinewood's no good. All she has to do is move her elbows and the sides will cave in."

'At the finish we buried her stood up in some greaseproof paper. Afterwards, my father ran off with a detective who'd come up on the pools. It was a bitter blow to me, because I'd never won anything.

'The crunch came when, after standing near a busy road for an hour, I was clamped. It was the last straw. I fled into Sherwood Forest and became an outlaw. It wasn't much fun, though, doing outlaw things on my own. I mugged one traveller, and when I saw how little he'd got in his wallet, I finished up letting him mug me!

'So I opened my shop, and I was doing very nicely, not making a fortune, you understand, but selling a few frocks, and I passed an audition for *Fiddler on the Roof.* Then Prince John started coming into the shop, buying lacy bits for some widow he was seeing in Newark. I always gave him a good discount but he got greedy, wanted the merchandise for virtually nothing, and so I advertised for some outlaws at the local job centre, and that's how the Merry Men started.'

'Is it true that you rob from the rich to give to the poor?' my mother asked sharply.

Robin shook his head. 'No. That's a load of cobblers. It's not good business, you see. No return on your investment.'

My mother stood up then and, with a note of controlled anger in her voice, she said, 'Mr Robinsky, I don't think you have any scruples.'

Whereupon Robin replied, 'I have a full set, I assure you, but having children isn't everything.'

When he had gone back into the forest deep, Mother turned to me. 'You'll regret it if you go off with that herbert. He won't amount to anything, and he'll probably end up on the scaffold.' But I didn't listen, did I? A month later I was in bed with him every night, and washing his smalls every day.

The first thing that got on my nerves was his untidiness. Arrows left on the three-piece suite, swords and bags of coins stuffed in our wardrobe. And he was out every Friday night, guzzling mead with the Merry Men, then coming home and trying to have it away with me. I didn't mind to begin with, but he used to get so pissed he had brewer's droop . . . And he was never at home. If it wasn't the shop, it was out ambushing people. The kitchen window was my world. Then he joined the golf club, and that did it. I went home to Mother.

'I told you so,' she said. 'Men are just hairy beasts, all after one thing.'

My guardian asked me outright, was it true that I knew Robin Hood? Well, what could I say? It was silly to deny it, because everybody knew I was his woman.

'Prince John's offering a big reward for the capture of your boyfriend,' my guardian murmured thoughtfully. 'Tell me, Marian. Do you love this outlaw, or is it merely the discount on the frocks that attracts you?'

I thought it over, and I really wasn't sure. You see, Robin was such a mean little bugger. He was doing very well out of robbing people and the shop was bringing in a few bob too, but he wouldn't spend a penny more than he had to. My kitchen was a disgrace and I badly needed a new Ewbank for the stairs. Would he buy me one? Not on your life. He was so mean, he took the pendulum off the grandfather clock, in case its shadow wore a hole in the wallpaper. He was so tight he started buying waterproof teabags. He used to sit for hours, sewing minced meat together to make a joint. I'd had enough of it, and so I arranged to have him trapped by Prince John's men.

The troops surrounded the shop that Wednesday, which should have been half-day closing, but not for Robinsky. Oh, no. He believed in staying open all the time to get the best possible profit. Profit to spend on what? I wanted to know. (The annual dinner dance was coming up, and I didn't have a decent rag to wear, and I felt so ashamed, walking about the camp in old Harris tweed ponchos and second-hand chastity belts.) Prince John's soldiers waited outside to keep the Merry Men back, but they'd all gone to a Ban the Crossbow demonstration in Bognor anyway. All the soldiers had to do was grab Robin and bung him in a dungeon until he saw the error of his ways and gave me more camp-keeping money. Not a difficult task, you would think.

But my plan failed. At the very moment that Prince John was storming the shop, my guardian, the Sheriff of Nottingham, strolled by.

'Hello, Johnny,' he said. 'What are you doing here?'

The Prince sniffed. 'Arresting Robinsky for high treason and overcharging on his VAT.'

My guardian looked a bit put out. 'That's a pity,' he mused. 'He's just finishing off a suit for me.'

Prince John looked at him, puzzled, like. 'But he's a ladies' tailor!'

My guardian wagged his digit coyly. 'That's what everybody thinks, but for a year or two he had a gents' outfitters in Golders Green.'

'Well, bless my fairly well-off soul,' replied the Prince. 'I've always admired the cut of your doublet and hose, but I thought you went to Savile Row.'

'Good grief!' my guardian laughed. 'I wouldn't pay their prices, even if I could afford it.' With that, the two men disappeared into the shop.

I followed close behind, for I wanted to see the look on Robin's face when he was arrested. This is what occurred . . .

'Listen here, Robinsky,' the Prince thundered. 'I want you to make me an outfit that will be the talk of the Court. Something very special. If not, I'll have you flung into my deepest dungeon without a shirt to your back or a roof to your mouth. Is that clearly understood, or would you like me to sing it in Latin?'

Robin simply shrugged his thin shoulders and said confidently, 'My dear Prince, for you I shall make a suit that, my life, it will be a tone poem in cloth. First, I will employ a team of aboriginal acrobats from east Tasmania, and then I'll rent a trampoline from a friend I know who runs a leisure centre and hand-relief massage clinic for the elderly, and then I'll ship them all off to Nepal in the Himalayas. The trampoline will be

stretched between two mountain peaks, and the acrobats
will wait until the very rare spotted lesser crested treble-
horned Kabul goat leaps from one peak to the other. All
eyes must be ready for this . . . it's peak viewing. When
the goat leaps, the acrobats, who by this time will have
formed a human pyramid, will jump up, and the man on
the top will grab handfuls of wool from around the
goat's inside thighs.

'The next step is to send a team of Polynesian oyster
divers to a remote island near Java. From the seabed,
they'll bring up several large electric eels. The sinews
from the eels' knees will make the thread to sew the wool
together. While we have the oyster divers with us, we'll
get them to dive into an underground cave off the coast
of Japan for some of the wide-lipped middle-aged non-
abrasive hermit clams that live in the middle of squids'
heads. The semi-precious silver mucus inside the clams
will be spin-dried and ironed into an unbreakable
material to make the buttons for your suit, dear Prince.'

Here, Robin paused for breath. Then he continued,
'Next we'll require a lining. For that we need the freshly
shaved skin off a polar bear's backside, and the only
place to obtain that is the North Pole. Now, polar bears
are difficult to find, because it's chilly up there, and they
don't go out a lot, unless it's for a birthday treat, so we'll
employ a team of O-level Eskimos on sick-leave to catch
one for us. You see, polar bears are very fond of
processed peas, so the Eskimos empty a tin of these
around a hole in the ice. When the polar bear comes out
for a pea, they kick it in the icehole. It takes about an
hour to shave the bear's bum, and when that's been
accomplished, a Harley Street surgeon is brought over
by recorded delivery. He peels away the top layer of skin
from its behind, paints it with tincture of iodine and
covers it with a plaster.

'Then the materials are shipped to a remote mill in

Oldham where, under the gaze of a team of specialists, the wool is woven on a laser loom and the lining's stitched in by microtechnology. Finally, the suit is parcelled up and sent to a high-class Chinese laundry, where it is ironed carefully. So secret is the identity of the suit's owner that, once it's ironed, the coolies involved are either beheaded on the spot or given a lease on a restaurant in Wardour Street.'

By the time he'd finished, most of the soldiers were asleep. Prince John, however, was in raptures. 'It sounds great, Robbie. When can I have it?' And Robin said, 'Tomorrow?'

It was a crap joke, even for Robin, and I knew he'd lost all hope of a pantomime that year.

Of course, Robin wasn't hustled away to a dungeon, and he took his revenge on me by cutting my family allowance.

But this was by no means by biggest problem with life in Sherwood Forest. More worrying was the lack of sanitation. There was no privacy whatsoever, and I was sick of having to crouch behind a clump of groundsel for a number two while bloody arrows whistled over my bonnet. It wasn't just the lack of privacy or the shortage of toilet tissue . . . after a meal of cabbage or sprouts or haricot beans, the pong was atrocious, and I found several rabbits gassed.

Worse was to follow. That eating machine, Friar Tuck, started bringing in take-away curries for the lads. Imagine it! The hot sun, filtering through the trees, and the men of Sherwood lifting their nether limbs to release the gases manufactured with the help of a good old-fashioned Madras and pilau rice. It was terrible. Soon, birds no longer sang in the trees, squirrels ran from their hiding-places wearing oxygen masks, and forest dwellers were using wild pig-shit indoors as air fresheners.

Mind you, going back to Nottingham Castle every other night was getting on my nerves too. If I missed the last late-night coach I had an hour's walk before hitting the main road. And when I got to the castle, my guardian was always going on about getting Prince John on the throne of England and his ambition to be the Prince's right-hand man and qualify for a free fortnight at a holiday camp and tickets to the Wimbledon jousting finals.

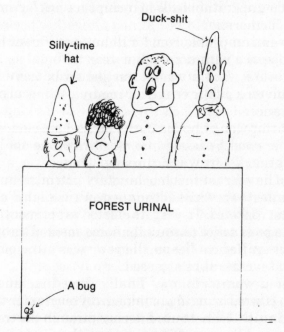

FOREST URINAL

Four of the merry men having a pee, prior to a pitched battle. This sketch by courtesy of the Cornball Friends of Suet and Imagination in Croydon. They say a Miss Amelia does a turn there with an onion and a wax clock, if she gets out of breath welding a fox cub to a pianist.

One day, I decided to take the bull by the horns, and asked Robin point-blank if he intended to marry me or not. He hummed and hawed, tried to fondle my bosom, and I kicked him in the balls.

About this time, even Robin's supporters in Nottingham were getting fed up with the smell coming from Sherwood. The Health Authorities were inundated by complaints, and a few days later the forest was invaded by hundreds of men in white overalls carrying buckets of disinfectant.

An organization called Greenpeace put forward a bill that curries should be banned altogether because non-curry-eating people could still get gas if confined in a small space with a person eating a vindaloo. Anyone who broke wind after ten pm should be heavily fined and given a public enema. Of course, the local criminal masterminds grabbed this chance of making money, and before long bootleg curries were being smuggled in from across the border. Gang wars broke out between black-market fruit and fibre mobsters.

People started bribing lavatory attendants, so they could get to the front of the queue. Prices for prunes and curries rocketed. Teenagers started experimenting with senna pods and Epsom salts; some smoked the mixture, others sniffed it. The smell grew worse, and old people longed for the days of good clean horse-shit.

The government was finally forced to take action when citizens started to complain of severe constipation, and Prince John started conscription in order to raise an army big enough to clear out the forest and close down the fart bunkers.

Robin told me he'd have to disappear for a while, and for once I agreed with him. So he rode off, leaving me in charge of the shop, would you believe? Business was quite good whilst the forest was being cleared out, but once the army and sanitation men left, things hit rock-bottom. And when the news hit town that Richard the Lionheart was on his way back home from God knows where, the recession bit deep. Prince John was bad, but Richard was a bloody sight worse. In the past, the newspapers had been full of his scandalous activities with choirboys and ambitious backbenchers, and he'd cost the country dear with his endless, brainless Crusades against Saledin.

As if that wasn't enough, my guardian was trying to marry me off. First, he tried to match me with Sir Gaspar Gwain-Humbold, who had a pre-fab castle in Yorkshire that was being re-mortgaged with the Abbey National. He was about five foot three on a good day, bald as a coot and couldn't pee. Then along came Squire Haddock. He was over seventy and hadn't had an erection since his mother first bathed him. My guardian even tried to pair me off with his nibs, Prince John, but honestly, girls, he bored the knickers off me.

So things were a bit slow, you might say. Robin away, the shop doing badly and not a whiff of romance in the air . . . until I met my knight in shining armour.

I'll never forget that morning. I'd been doing the washing down at the river, and I was just about to spin-dry a load when I heard a horse neighing. I looked round as a knight rode into view. Girls, my heart fluttered like a butterfly trapped inside a jam jar! He was tall, fair and slim, with a hidden strength about his bearing. His eyes were blue saucers of confident clarity and his armour shone with numerous coats of Pledge polish. In his hand he carried a lance with a pennant flying from it . . . I fell in love just looking at him.

He dismounted and clanked towards me, and suddenly I was in his arms, sucking the rivets on his jacket. In silence, he handed me a spanner and I began to undo the bolts that held his armour together.

I had a spot of trouble with the Philip's screwdriver,

because the chain-mail round his armpits had rusted, so I had to send for a welding set and goggles. Then I had difficulty getting his metal boots off. The top plates of his armour had been badly fitted and some self-tapping screws were cross-threaded. I'd need a high-speed hand-operated drill to remove those. By the time I'd done that it was two days later, and I still hadn't managed to loosen his stainless-steel codpiece.

Finally, I got him down to his vest and Y-fronts, but I'd lost the lust, as it were. And so I remained true to Robin Hood after all.

My knight in shining armour turned out to be Sir Galahad, who was rather famous. Apparently, he and some other knights knocked about with this provincial twit who called himself King Arthur, or Arnold, I'm not sure which. You see, the main trouble with England was that there were dozens of dotty people who kept proclaiming themselves monarch of funny little places. I mean, the imbecile who lived round the corner from our Elsie's shop called himself the King of Mercia. I ask you! He hadn't got two castles to rub together, and his wife was a slut. Never once did I see her clean the bay window of their bungalow, and as for the state of her washing on the line!

Anyway, Sir Galahad and I had Bovril and crumpets, and while we were chatting, he mentioned that he and the other knights were looking for the Holy Grail. He asked me to keep an eye out for those antique roadshows that came round from time to time, and I said I would.

'Marian,' he said mid-crumpet, 'I do like this table.'

I nodded with satisfaction, for the table had once belonged to the Emir of Zanzadilothraserr, but he gave it up because he couldn't spell it. It was beautiful, perfectly round. Galahad said it was the sort of thing they could do with at Camelot, because at present they were using separate tables, and people weren't speaking to one another.

'I'm prepared to offer you a big bag of gold for it, Marian,' said Galahad, or Eric, as he liked to be known.

Well, it was too good an opportunity to miss. But I thought I'd better speak to Robin about it first.

I'd heard nothing from my little outlaw for a while, and I decided to smack his head the minute I got hold of him. Within a week or so, the so-called Merry Men arrived back at the camp and immediately started moaning on about inflation. It got on my pip and no mistake, and I flatly refused to MC their staff dances. Then, one late afternoon, Robin trooped up, and with him were the weirdest collection of people I've ever clapped eyes on. One of them stood the size of a small Alp, with a face like a bad cartoon (what really gave me the willies was the dwarf up his cardigan). One fellow had a bucket welded on his head, and another had so many pimples on his face he looked like a Lego advert. Only the man called Edmond Dantés seemed sane. Then the big chap, the one Robin called Walter the Moron, said, 'Hello, Marian. Do you know anybody that I can bounce? I'll give you a toffee, duck, before I'm sick in my hat.'

I'll keep away from that silly sod for a start, I thought. Where on earth had Robin met these oddballs? He'd only been away for three years.

A few days later, after I'd told Robin what I thought of him, an accountant was waylaid in the forest. Little John sensibly suggested that the prisoner looked through our books, to see how the shop was faring. I gave the man a goose-quill, and his writing was awful . . . mainly because the quill was still attached to the goose. The verdict was depressing. The shop was on the brink of financial disaster, and a bull terrier had chewed through six original ballgowns ordered by a Dutch woman who was living with a resident transvestite on a golf course.

Robin sat on a dead moose and sobbed. I had to be the strong one. After I'd introduced Sir Galahad, I told Robin about the table. Sir Galahad would give us enough gold to pay off the lease, send back the unsold stock and hire somebody to assassinate the bull terrier.

Reluctantly, Robin agreed, and Galahad rode away with the round table behind him, tied to his horse's tail. We shoved the gold into unit trusts, but kept a bit back for a new bathroom suite.

And so the days passed. Pimply Al spent hours with a hot towel on his face, unsuccessfully trying to get rid of his spots. Little John stole an Angus bull for Walter to bounce, which kept him happy, and the man with the bucket on his head developed metal fatigue in his ears. Pierre Le Toq wore a hunted expression, which you can buy in three colours from any decent chemist, and Mr Bovary competed with Allen a-Dale to see who could compose the nicest ode ... I must confess, I rather fancied getting Bovary between the sheets, but that's another story ...

Meanwhile, my guardian kept sending soldiers after the outlaws. Frankly, there was more chance of Preston getting back into the first division than the Sheriff capturing one of our gang. Prince John sent me a dead pygmy and a snake for my birthday ... and I made a very tasty snake and pygmy pie.

Life was simple in the forest deep. On Mondays there were lectures on various crab diseases and how to spot a phantom pregnancy in a tin of salmon. Tuesdays was usually a massed square dance and swim to the Orkneys. And on Wednesday mornings there were talks on how to stop a cavalry charge, using only a hairnet and some watercress. Thursdays, all day, we had a cold buffet in the tree-house, and I used to starch eggs to see if they could tell the time. There was always quite a bit of excitement on Fridays, when we had the Blow-up Doll

Puncture Repair Class. Most of the outlaws said the dolls made a change from sleeping with logs. Saturdays were when we made cathedrals out of matchsticks. These hand-crafted works of art would be exchanged for essentials, like dried mango root and pickled mongoose lips on a light bed of apricot balsawood. Sundays were given over to religious matters and, indeed, the pious old fraud Friar Tuck got stoned religiously. Some of the outlaws amused themselves by crossing a mole's leg and watching it whistle itself to sleep. Others read the papers, washed their feet and played *Name That Tune* inside a sack of warm truffles. As for Robin and I, we tried to make love in a haywain, but some dirty sod was peeping at us between the pony's front legs . . . which is a pretty rotten way for a pony to get its kicks.

One day a recorded delivery parchment arrived from Sir Galahad. He said that the table was a great success, and King Arthur seemed a much better chap now. We were all invited to the Court of Camelot for a hot-pot supper, with a charity joust with latex lances and a troupe of eel jugglers from Gravesend.

Meanwhile, Prince John had heard that King Richard was back in England, and would be popping in to see Robin and the Merry Men as soon as he'd done his shopping in Harrods. My guardian wasn't sure which side to support, so he resigned as Sheriff of Nottingham, and obtained a job as assistant musical co-ordinator with the Scarborough Tourist Board and Fish-Manure Dye Works.

At once Prince John and his soldiers started watching every path into Sherwood Forest, in case King Richard attempted to reach our camp. But the Prince had reckoned without the woman who was to change the course of English history, Florence the Whore, who, at that very moment, was approaching the forest, still carrying her unborn child.

Although I had never met Florence, the tales of her ugliness chilled my blood. Somewhere in my heart, however, I sympathized with her. After all, had she not been brutally abused?

An arrow flashed through the air – a signal from one of the sentries on duty up a spruce tree. It told us that a large fat crone was shuffling through the trees towards us. Pierre started whimpering like a nervous infant so, to stop him running away, Walter bounced him into a packing crate with a boiled ham sandwich and a carton of double cream.

Meanwhile, we all waited with baited breath. Would Florence reach the centre of the forest deep? Or would Prince John's men nab her first?

The sound of running feet gave us the answer . . . well, that and muffled shouts such as, 'Take your hands off my tights!' or 'Bloody hell! It's the creature from the black lagoon!'

Within fifteen minutes two hundred soldiers ran into our camp, all of them waving white flags. Some of them wanted to join the Merry Men, and others wanted to join the British Legion. There was a brief fight, but

Sheriff of Nottingham and Prince John doing a blackfaced minstrel act for Comic Relief in the Civic Hall, Dewsbury, when it was raining. Jokes about duck-shit went down well.

little Quasimodo more or less took on the lot of them while Robin and the Merry Men went ten-pin bowling.

Then Florence came into view. The mere thought of Pierre making love to her sent me running for a sedative. She really was as ugly as sin. And yet she had some things which men might desire – muscles like gammon steaks, an intriguing duelling scar and a montage of bright tattoos down her iron-hard thighs.

Pierre stood before her, begging forgiveness, but Florence seemed strangely uninterested. She was gazing intently at Walter the Moron, and he was gazing intently back. There and then, in that forest glade, a love story blossomed between a most unlikely couple.

Nine months later Florence pushed a 17lb baby boy into this vale of tears; the babe already showed signs of needing a shave. Walter and Florence left Sherwood Forest shortly afterwards, and don't think they didn't make a handsome couple, because they didn't. We gave them a few presents and Quasimodo made an awfully boring speech. Pierre was so grateful for his narrow escape that he vowed eternal allegiance to Robin Hood. A few weeks later King Richard got back on the throne, threw away his summer frocks and promised to be a good lad, and not mince about Soho on Friday nights. Prince John went back to Runnymede, where he tried to invent double-glazing.

As for Robin and me, Maid Marian, we got planning permission to open a swimming-bath, but Robin wouldn't take the plunge. Financially, he said, we'd be out of our depth. Well, I went off the deep end and told him I couldn't fathom him out, and our relationship took a dive. There was even a column about us, splashed across the front page of the local paper, but it was soon filtered out.

About the same time, four young cows fell into a watering hole and drowned. The heifers belonged to

Robin's brother-in-law, Hymie, and Allen a-Dale wrote a song about the incident, called 'Hymie's Four Heifers Blowing Bubbles'.

READERS' JOKE COMPETITION

Why did a morally and physically disturbed chicken cross the road on a day like Thursday, which I love and respect for coming after Wednesday, which is one son of a bitch...? Because it feels like a duck with too many feathers... it can't get up for down!

(This sophisticated joke was sent from New York in an airtight set of matching gherkins by Hank Panky, a veteran disc jockey in an oil works.

Mr Panky, who was the first American to balance a jugged hare in a funnel during a Dutch avalanche said from the canvas bag where he lives with his all-daughter euphonium rock band that he was very upset at being folded up the wrong way during a stocktaking jamboree. Our editor feels that Mr Panky is the man who made advances to his third wife's canary before going strange in a pen pal's duffle coat.)

FORWARD, DEAR READER ...

THE TESTIMONY OF
PIERRE LE TOQ: II

I cannot tell you what a relief it was to see Florence and Walter leaving Robin Hood's camp together. Oh, joy of joys!

Apart from the knowledge that I wouldn't have to fork out for the baby, I had developed a keen interest in Maid Marian. She was a nice-looking woman and very charming, although she did tend to take her teeth out and belch after a supper of venison pie and cabbage sauce. What she saw in Robinsky Hood, I'll never know. That shop was all he thought about and, like all the Merry Men, I was sick of modelling his damned frocks. It wasn't so bad for the others, they suited twin-sets and flounced underskirts, but my figure and delicate colouring would have been put to best advantage in a pair of flared slacks with a bolero jacket and layered silk blouse. The crunch came when he ordered me to model a full-length ribbed corset and elk-hide pantyhose with sequins. Of course, I flatly refused. I'd look ridiculous walking down the catwalk in front of all those ghastly retainers.

I decided I'd had enough of living in the forest. Robin took the news surprisingly well and paid me my wages for the overtime I'd put in, sewing up the crinoline dresses for the Merry Men's Hungarian Foxtrot Dancing Team, and Marian refused to do anything naughty with me behind the latrines. When I told Quasimodo that I was leaving, he decided to travel with me. He wanted to speak to Bonnie Prince Charlie, who was locked in his digs in Preston.

We made our goodbyes, and the Merry Men sang 'We'll Meet Again', then we headed north. We walked for many miles, each of us alone with our thoughts, and desperate for food. It was getting cold, and I felt a snowflake land on my nose. We would have to find shelter soon, because Quasimodo's arse was so close to the ground that if it snowed heavily his wedding tackle would freeze into a fossil.

As if in answer to my silent prayer, I saw a cave loom up before us. I picked the midget up and ran, reaching the cavern as the first bitter flurry of snow began its maddened fandango.

I found some dried twigs and started a small fire, whilst Quasimodo pulled what little food we had left from our haversacks. There wasn't much . . . just half a goose with mixed pickles, three large cod steaks in batter, two bottles of brandy and a ham shank in glazed aspic and basil. Apart from a packet of crisps, all that was left in the bag was a table, two chairs and a St Bernard pup . . . We had a long night ahead of us.

Somehow we slept in that cold hard cave, even though we only had six blankets between us. I let Quasimodo have the hot-water bottle for his little feet, and wrapped a thermal shirt round my own footsies.

It was deep in the middle of the night when our rest was interrupted. I cannot say how long we slumbered, because I didn't have a tape-measure, but I felt about the same height. Suddenly, a tall man in a cape, Inverness see-through gaiters and a piano accordion jumped into view.

'Hello, and welcome to the Cave! Yes, folks, it's cabaret time once again . . . so put your hands together

for that great wit from Stratford upon the jolly old
Avon . . . Willy Make 'em Laugh Shakespeare!'

The compère hopped off the stage, playing 'Happy
Days Thou Art Here Again', to be replaced by a medium-
sized man with a bald head and trim moustache,
wearing quite an expensive doublet and hose. He bowed
to us and started his performance:

'Good evening, gentleman and ladies . . . that does it,
next time I'll rehearse the act.

I wouldn't say my wife's fat, but that's what she's
got . . . a fat butt. On the night we were married and I
carried her over the threshold, I had to make three
trips.

Marriage is a compromise. Like the time the wife
wanted a fur coat and I wanted a second-hand horse.
Well, folks, we couldn't afford both, so we compromised
. . . she got the coat, but we keep it in the stables.

Last Christmas my wife said to me, "We're having
mother up for dinner." I said, "Great, kiddo. She'll
make a change from turkey."

Her mother is so ugly the milkman flirts with
me . . . I've never seen a woman eat so fast . . . she
even has spark plugs on the cruet. And is that dame
dumb? The other day I said to her that I was
collecting for Queen Elizabeth's trust fund . . . She
said, "I didn't know she was ruptured."'

When he'd finished, Quasimodo and I gave him a
rousing cheer, and asked him to join us at our rock for a
drink. We told him that we thought he was funny, and
what a pity it was that there wasn't a bigger audience.
He just shrugged, and said that business had been crap
for some time. Willy was great company, and soon
Quasimodo and I were telling him about our adventures.
He was fascinated, and asked if he could take notes.

'I'm sick of doing stand-up comedy,' he said. 'Too much travel, going from gig to gig. Last week I died at Camelot. Oh, you've heard of it? Well, I tell you, if any comic can get a laugh from those miserable sods, he's entitled to a fortnight's holiday in Malta. I played the Court once, told my naughty joke about a Knight's Templar and an Arab vibrator, and they docked my money and threatened me with the stocks. I'm thinking of giving it all up and becoming a writer. You know, plays and things? If I jot down all the strange stories I hear, like the ones you've been telling me tonight, I'll soon have all the material I need.' Then he shook our hands and left, leaving Quasimodo and me to get some more sleep.

The following day we met a farmer. He was in a haycart drawn by a depressed-looking donkey, but for a piffling sum he agreed to give us a lift to Manchester. I'd never been in the North of England before, and what I saw I didn't like. It was raining buckets, footpads abounded and the streets were piled high with horse-shit. Ah, how it reminded me of my native land! Oh, I missed my beloved France. In my mind's eye I could see the Rue Pigalle on a Saturday night . . . the wine . . . *les femmes . . . la pox . . .*

It was in a dark inn in Salford that Quasimodo and I were to uncover a plot so sinister, so far-fetched, it sounds bloody stupid, which it is, of course, but what the hell! It makes a rattling good yarn!

We had taken two trollops into this inn. My doxy was a bold, black-haired gypsy from Warrington, while my friend courted a six-foot-two-inch stripper from Hamburg. She'd brought a rope ladder, so that Quasimodo could climb up beyond her knees.

Well, we drank heartily and roughly caressed our ladies of the night. My slut had thighs like gammon steaks and her breasts were so big she wore mud flaps on her nipples. Quasimodo had crawled up inside his ladyfriend's vest, and her eyes bore testimony to what the little sod was up to.

At that precise moment, just as lust was overpowering my senses, a man slipped into our cubicle. 'Please, sir. You have the face of a kind man. Please help me. The authorities are after me. If they approach, will you say that I have been with you all evening?' He seemed all right, so I said, 'Certainly. You want me to provide you with an alibi?'

He shook his head. 'No thanks, but I'll have a gin and orange.' Then he stopped talking as the curtain of our cubicle was swept back, and we were confronted by three burly men.

'How long have you been in this tavern, my good sir?' one of them asked sternly. I said that we five had been in the inn since it opened. One of the men lifted an eyebrow and snarled, 'Thou cannot count numbers, sir. I see only four of you.'

I couldn't resist. I shouted, 'Come out, Quasimodo!' and the midget squirmed out from under the stripper's vest with a dreamy look on his face.

'You really are Quasimodo, the greatest swordsman in all Europe! Please forgive this intrusion, gentlemen, and carry on with your pleasures. We seek a vile traitor. His name is Guy Fawkes.' With that, they left us alone. It didn't take a genius to figure out that our new-found companion was the mysterious Guy Fawkes.

'Thank you for shielding me. It was kind of you. Yes, I am wanted by the authorities, but I swear to you that I am innocent.' He paused and sipped his gin and orange, then, as my bold gypsy did some wonderful things under my codpiece . . . I was merely a prawn in her hands . . . he told us his story.

'When I was but a stripling, I met a Chinaman who owned a café in Lambeth, and he taught me the secret of making decent fireworks in return for getting him an audition at the Palladium. At this point, perhaps I should say that I was abandoned by my mother. She left me on so many doorsteps, I used to call a pint of skimmed milk "Daddy". My childhood is a dream to me now, but I vaguely remember having some sisters, although I can't be sure . . .

'Well, in time I opened a little business, hiring out firework displays for children's parties or birthday celebrations, you know, all that sort of thing. I was in great demand and seriously thinking about expanding, even taking on more staff, preferably non-union. Then one night I was approached by a couple of high-ranking men, or at least that's what they seemed, who said there was going to be a big party in the Houses of Parliament, and they wanted me to provide special loud bangers and extra gunpowder-filled rip-raps. I readily agreed – this was an important booking, one that could lead to a summer season in Bournemouth.

'I followed my instructions carefully. I had to keep the whole thing a secret, and so I crept into the cellars with my barrels of gunpowder, paper hats and novelty teeth, coloured streamers and rubber Mucky Pup. I was ready for the party, all right, but then some guards arrived and I was arrested. Luckily I had some gunpowder in my pocket, so I blasted the cell door open and fled . . . and that is the truth of the matter, sirs.'

I patted him on the shoulder. 'The Watch will not take you,' I said. 'You are safe with us.'

He asked if I'd like his card, in case we ever fancied a night out or needed any fireworks for a works outing. As he drew some pieces of paper from his pockets, out tumbled a drawing of none other than Florence!

'Do you know this person?' I gasped.

He nodded. 'Well, frankly, I am told she is my mother, although I find it hard to believe. She is so ugly, the sight of her churns my bowels and causes me to trump.'

This news changed everything and, slipping two gold sovereigns apiece down their blouses, Quasimodo told the whores to leave us at once. They tap-danced out of the room to the sound of a Swiss sailor yodelling the 'Trumpet Voluntary' and drinking a glass of water at the same time. I was sorry to see them go, but Fate had dealt us another hand in this strange game called Life . . .

So Florence had spawned Guy Fawkes! I had a feeling that history would remember this name.

'You said that you thought you had sisters?' I said to Guy. 'Were you the only son?'

Guy Fawkes paled. 'I have not told you the whole story, good sirs. There was no son, for I am of the female sex.'

Quasimodo and I sat back, stunned by this new revelation. Seeing the disbelief on our faces, Guy Fawkes removed his beard and moustache, then his pantaloons and shirt, and now stood before us . . . a very pretty woman.

'Pray do not reveal my secret to the Sunday papers, I beg you,' he/she said, and we nodded.

'You must stay with us,' Quasimodo said gently.

Guy then explained that his real name was Irene, shoved his false hair back on his head and bought us three pints of mild and bitter each, and a Campari and soda for himself.

What we had heard and seen that night had taken our breath away, and as we stood in the street, waiting for a coach, we were brutally attacked by six powerful men, who threw sacks over our heads, dragged us into a dark alleyway and clubbed us. All I remember is the swish of the cudgel and the sharp smell of fresh horse-shit, then a pit of blackness swallowed me up.

I awoke with a splitting headache, unable to move.

Gradually, my vision cleared and, to my surprise, I saw that I was lying in a large ornate bed, and my hands and feet were tied to each of the four posts. Over by the fireplace, Quasimodo had been jammed into a coal-scuttle, and Guy Fawkes was chained to the wall. Before I could speak, the doors of the chamber were thrown open. I thought I'd lost my reason when I saw who walked in – Henry the Eighth. He came to the foot of the bed and began to untie me. Soon all three of us were free. The King indicated that we should sit down and a manservant gave us all a cup of Earl Grey tea.

'Now then, you scallywags, which of you is the real Guy Fawkes?' the King said softly.

'I am, your Majesty,' Guy replied in a trembling voice.

The King nodded and said, 'I believe you have in your possession a sketch of someone I might know.'

In silence, Guy handed the drawing of foul Florence to King Henry. The monarch pored over it, his face a mass of conflicting emotions. Then with a wave of his hand he dismissed his retinue and we were alone.

'Guy Fawkes – or may I call you Irene?' King Henry said tremulously.

Guy Fawkes gasped and went as white as a length of Bury tripe. 'How do you know?'

King Henry placed his hands on Guy's shoulders and kissed him full on the lips. 'I know because I am your elder sister Madge . . . Florence was my mother too, dear sister.'

To say that we were taken aback is an understatement. Henry the Eighth, now Madge, threw off his clothes, and all at once I realized why he always looked so big. Underneath his men's clothing he wore a skirt and Fair Isle jumper, nicely complementing a two-strand pearl necklace and matching earrings – I thought the high-heeled shoes were a bit off the wall, though.

Guy took off his men's clothes and the two ladies

stood there, crying on each other's shoulders and kissing passionately. At once, Quasimodo and I vowed to help these ladies find their sisters and their mother.

The four of us crept out of St James's Court and found digs in Hammersmith. The next morning we put an ad in the papers, which read simply: Any friend of Flo is a friend we'd like to contact.'

Frankly, we didn't expect any replies, but within three days we picked up a paper and read: 'Must talk about F. Very important. Signed H.'

We were all very excited by this and, throwing caution to the winds, held a party in our flat. It cost a few quid, but Madge got the mead cheap, Irene fixed up some Catherine-wheels and we all played Monopoly. Our guests had only just departed when we heard the sound of running feet. Soldiers! We had been betrayed!

Almost without thinking, we climbed out through the skylight, leaving Quasimodo to mount a rearguard action, and giving us time to make good our escape. As we crawled along the ridged roof towards a flight of stairs leading to the street below, we heard the clash of steel and cries of pain as the soldiers felt the might of Quasimodo's blade. Then we waited anxiously for our friend, who soon appeared, wiping the blood from his sword.

We spent that night in a park, discussing the best way to avoid capture. Suddenly Quasimodo slapped his thigh and pointed to a sign which read: 'This Way for the Greatest Show on Earth – the René Claubert Show!'

I could have kissed the midget. Of course! No one would think of looking for us in a freak show.

The next morning, Quasimodo and I visited Claubert in his small tented arena at the far end of the park. We were welcomed with open arms. Quasimodo told the showman everything and begged for his help.

'Alas, my friend,' Claubert said, as he watched an

octopus playing with a set of bagpipes and getting nowhere. 'I no longer have a freak show. All I exhibit now are wax statues of famous people.'

Quasimodo looked at me. I looked at him. Claubert looked at both of us. The same idea flashed through all our minds. Quickly, I tore a large branch from a poplar tree and strode over to where the tub of wax sat, smouldering over a gentle fire. Scooping up a big dollop of the viscous stuff, I smeared it over Quasimodo's face.

'Who would you like him to be?' I asked Claubert.

He scratched his chin reflectively. 'Try a small Richard the Third.'

I daubed a lump of wax on to Quasimodo's nose, moulding it into a long hook, then placed a big splodge of the stuff on to his back, rounding it to form a hump.

'My God,' said Claubert emotionally, shaking me warmly by the hand. 'He looks just like a miniature Laurence Olivier.'

We supped on fresh bread and wine that night. I love warm freshly baked bread. It fills a knead in me. In France most young soldiers, the flour of our country, are brought up on bread, and each one plays his roll. I've always proposed a toast to bread; in fact, I proposed one only yeasterday. Even the poor, who can get crusty when there's no dough, know that in the desert a Frenchman will never starve – there's always plenty of sandwiches.

Ah, yes! Our little band ate well, and as we lay under the stars my thoughts were of my dear parents. They met when Father had gone to place a large money wager on a horse. He saw my mother's long blonde hair glinting in the sunshine and, on impulse, tugged at a strand and wrapped it round a banknote for luck. Mother did not take offence. Instead, she poured Dad a large brandy to further his fortune . . . the horse won. They got married and kept up the tradition of using brandy and my mother's hair for luck at every race meeting for over thirty years. I remember them both at their Golden Wedding . . . you couldn't mistake them . . . she was bald and he was pissed.

Gradually sleep overtook me, and as I fell into a dreamless slumber I wondered what tomorrow would bring. We would need all our strength, that was certain, for when one is week, one is in a day's. Still, we were alive, and it was not a time for morning.

The next evening, René Claubert's show had some new attractions – Henry the Eighth, Guy Fawkes and Tom Thumb. As for myself, I remained in the background. For it was my job to dip my friends into the hot wax, and to ensure they stood perfectly still on stage. They were an instant hit with the public. One night, some soldiers came in and roared their approval. There was one sticky moment when a trooper pushed a doughnut on to Henry's nose, but he kept still and the soldier soon got bored and went away. A week later we moved the show to Oldham, but it was shut. In Blackburn we had another nasty incident. A young frump put her hand inside Quasimodo's trousers and yelled, 'Eeh bah gum, Fred. This little wax dummy's dick's gone hard.'

Luckily, Fred was as thick as pig-shit, and he just said, 'Well, it's bound to be, you daft-head. Wax does go hard after a bit.'

Generally, business was rather slow in Blackburn and at my suggestion we set forth for Preston, where we hoped to make contact with the Bonnie Prince.

Funny town, Preston turned out to be. There was so much pollution in the atmosphere, if you threw a ball up into the air, it stayed there. I've never seen so much soot . . . even the birds flew about with bottles of Optrex. We found Bonnie Prince Charlie eventually, in a bed and breakfast near the station. He looked really fed up.

Nobody had rallied to his cause, and there was nothing at the job centre. His loyal soldiers had got sick of people looking up their kilts, and a lot of them had gone home for Easter.

'Quite honestly, I think I've dropped rather a big brick with this marching down to London idea. There seems to be so much indifference to politics here. The only thing they care about in Preston is whippet racing. It's very depressing.' He stopped talking and sliced a raw bloater, throwing half to the Indian Parrot standing on his head.

Suddenly I saw Madge and Irene staring intently at the Prince. I wondered why at first, then I saw the family resemblance . . .

Madge stood up, removed her whiskers and boomed, 'You are not Bonnie Prince Charlie. He doesn't exist, does he? If I'm correct, and I feel sure that I am, you are Beryl . . . and I am your elder sister Madge.'

'Oh, thank heavens I can be myself again,' Beryl cried, her face full of joy and relief. Then she turned to Irene, who smiled gently and whispered, 'I am your sister Irene. Yes, my dear, Florence was our mother too.'

I had to chip in at this juncture. 'But why did Florence bring you up as boys?'

They all shook their heads, had another good cry and compared make-up. When they'd all calmed down a bit, Bonnie Prince Charlie (or rather, Beryl) told his story. Meanwhile, he knitted himself a housecoat. (I should have said 'her' story, but what the hell!)

'All I remember is being taken to Scotland and left with a nutcase called Robert the Bruce. All he was interested in was bloody spiders, his manners were atrocious and he was continually pissed. Apparently, he'd given the English a bit of a clobbering, so all his mates thought he was great.

'"The day will come, young lady," my nurse used to

say, "when you will lead Scotland to greatness." But I never took much notice, because I didn't play rugby. It wasn't easy, as I'm sure Madge and Irene will testify, passing myself off as a boy. When my tutor said, "You've got no balls for playing cricket," he little realized how close he was to the truth.

'Anyway, the next thing is, I'm fitted out with sword and shield, bunged on a horse and told to ride south. I'll never forget that day. Flora MacDonald, a good friend of mine who's in on the secret, saw me off one chilly dawn, with a flask of tea and some McVitie's biscuits. It took ages to get through England. Nobody took any notice of us, not even when we snarled and waved our claymores at them.

'Wednesday was half-day closing, you see, and we got stopped time after time by vicars asking us to open garden fêtes.

'Finally I reached Preston and, as you can see, here the dream came to an end. All is lost for Scotland – but at least I've been reunited with two of my sisters.'

We played Preston for over three weeks and soon Beryl had made enough money to give the Scottish troops their wages. Some of the men went straight home, and a few went to try for a part in *Brigadoon*.

We'd forgotten all about the newspaper ad, so it was a shock when, on our last night in Preston, a man, obviously a mariner, visited my caravan.

'It has taken me a long time to find you,' he said. 'Allow me to introduce myself. My name is Hardy. Nelson's best mate.'

I wondered what he was after, and as if he had read my mind, the newcomer went on, 'Before Horatio popped his clogs, he said, "Hardy, old man, find my mother. Her name is Florence and I am her eldest daughter." Of course, I thought he'd gone round the twist. Seeing my expression, Horatio whispered, "It's true, pull down my pants."

'Well, I did just that, sir, and it *was* true: Admiral Lord Horatio Nelson was a rather hairy lady and her real name was – Ethel.

'As you can imagine, good sirs, I was stunned. There we were, lying on the blood-stained deck and Lord Nelson with his trousers round his ankles. Snide comments flew at us, fast and furious: "Bloody arse bandits", "Dirty old men", "Should be hung from the yardarm, the filthy sodomites" . . . Around us the battle was still raging as I pulled up Horatio's pants. "Now do you believe me, dear heart?" he whispered, and attempted to dab on some lipstick. "I really am a woman. Hardy, don't let the world know about my sex, will you? Mummy wanted me to be a man, and I want her to know that I died a man." He coughed and drew heavily on his Balkan Sobranie. "If you can, Hardy," he said, "let her know that I died a hero. The last I heard, she was working as a butcher in Harrogate. Her name is Florence." With that, we lost him. He hadn't died, we just lost him. Luckily I found him just before he fell over the side of the ship, and he expired in my arms. So ended the life of one of England's great and noble heroes, Horatio Nelson . . . But to me he will always be Ethel.'

The news that yet another of Florence's daughters had been tracked down was staggering, and I was beginning to feel more than a passing respect for the mysterious whore of Paris. Had she not given the world four daughters who, posing as men, had changed the shape of history?

The ladies and I camped outside Blackpool, and I must confess, somewhat shamefaced, that I started having affairs with *les girls*. Oh, I know I should not have done so, but the weather was getting warmer, the sap was rising and it was such a thrill to be humping a girl who used to be, say, Guy Fawkes (Irene was always booked for Tuesday mornings). Can you imagine the strangeness of foreplay with a passionate woman who was once Henry the Eighth?

One night, whilst practising the rhythm method, Beryl (Bonnie Prince Charlie) broke down in tears. 'We simply have to find our mother,' she wept. The rest of us agreed . . . but where to look?

It was Irene who suggested asking the Knights of the Round Table. Good, sound thinking, I thought. The knights rode all over the country, prodding people with their lances, and looking for a Holy Grail or whatever, and getting decorators' quotes for refurbishing Camelot. They were bound to have heard of Florence on their travels.

I found a mule of long measurement, which we could all ride on. We called it 'riding in tandem'. That sort of rejoinder comes in a cycle and I said it because I was the spokesman. Not wanting to be saddled with a pun like that, I back-pedalled quickly and chained the subject. Later, we met a lot of sheep crowding the roads, not that it bothered me. I'm always ready to handle baas.

However, it proved to be a long journey, and over the days the girls got cross. Irene said she'd missed a period, and I got bothered. At any rate, it took us two months to reach Camelot, and by that time we were all so hungry, we ate the mule . . . delicious with anchovies and whipped cream.

Well, I for one found Camelot most disappointing. Unlike French castles, it was built in a hollow, and it was made of cardboard and – yes, you've guessed it, you astute reader, you – compressed horse-shit. There was an empty moat round the castle . . . King Arthur had forgotten to pay his water rates. The battlements were smeared with jam stains, where bored soldiers had been eating butties on duty, and the stables were so filthy, the

horses followed one another with buckets! All the siege
catapults had frayed elastic bands, and there wasn't a
drop of boiling oil in the cauldrons. It was a mess and no
mistake. King Arthur turned out to be a doddering old
fool with loose dentures and prostate trouble. Guinevere,
his buxom wife, was having it away with Sir Lancelot
right under the King's runny nose, and the other
knights were always Brahms and Liszt.

They'd obviously used the Round Table for playing
nine-card brag, and the surface was all scratched and
marked, and it reeked of sour ale. They were kind
enough hosts, gave up their beds for us, but we had to
wash the bedding first. I found a dead flea in my
bed . . . that didn't worry me, but twenty thousand of its
relatives came to the funeral!

Friday night was a social evening. The knights hired
caterers and musicians and cabaret acts. Beryl, Irene
and Madge dolled themselves up and caused a flicker of
interest.

The food was crap. The wine wasn't too awful . . . but
in *la belle* France we'd have treated sewage with it.
Then the musicians came on, playing the harp and the
lyre. They were terrible . . . I won't harp on it, but I just
decided to string along, and that's the truth . . . I'm no
lyre, nor am I blowing my own trumpet, but music's a
cymbal to me . . . now where on earth did I drum that
one up from? At any rate, I'm not going to spinet out any
longer. Accordion to the others, I was acting as if I was
being entertained in a vile-inn.

After the music, we were served bread pudding and
coffee. King Arthur said a few words of welcome, then
sat down and called for a serf with a Red Cross diploma
to come and sluice out his bladder. Lancelot and the
Queen, meanwhile, were doing something rude with a
Cumberland sausage. When Arthur sat down, I stood up
and said a few choice words, but the knights simply

blew raspberries at me, shouting, 'Bleedin' Frog'. That angered me, for I could have toad them a thing or two.

At that moment the cabaret hopped on to the makeshift stage. It was the musicians again, and they seemed strangely familiar somehow. Actually, it wasn't a bad routine:

HIM: 'What do you get if you cross a hen with a dog?'
HER: 'I don't know, honeybunch. What do you get if you cross a hen with a dog?'
HIM: 'Are you ready for this, gorgeous? . . . You get a pooched egg! Ha, ha, ha.'
HER: 'That gag is so old it's had transplants and a facelift.'
HIM: 'What about you? You've had your face lifted so often, you talk through your navel.'
HER: 'You're so ugly, if you poke your head through a coach window, people think it's a cattle-truck . . . Boom-Boom.'

They didn't get many laughs, but I liked their ending. She picked up a bow and arrow and he stood on an apple, then she shot him off. That was when I recognized them . . . Maid Marian and Robin Hood.

After the show I went backstage to chew the fat, and got grease down my shirt. (It's strange how some people lean to fat.) Robin and Marian were delighted to see me, and they filled me in on all that had happened since Quasimodo and I had left the forest deep.

'The other outlaws left soon after you'd gone,' Robin said. 'There wasn't much to do and the lads wanted to try working inside for a bit. Little John got married, you know. He went on holiday to Stratford-upon-Avon and married some writer's housekeeper, Anne something . . . Hathaway.'

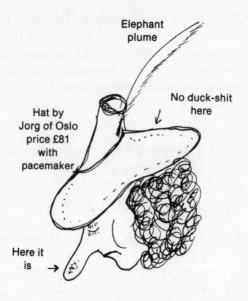

Elephant plume

No duck-shit here

Hat by Jorg of Oslo price £81 with pacemaker

Here it is →

Death mask of Maid Marian taken when she was
dead by someone who wasn't.

I staggered back. 'But this cannot be! Anne Hathaway
is William Shakespeare's girlfriend!'

Marian burst out laughing. 'You are such an innocent
sometimes, dear Pierre. There is no such person as
William Shakespeare . . . only Wilhelmina.'

I was thunderstruck, and it wasn't even raining. 'You
mean Shakespeare's a woman?'

Marian nodded. 'We go to the same hairdresser,
Michael's of Bond Street.'

It was imperative that the ladies and I talk to
Shakespeare as quickly as possible. Quasimodo, meanwhile, had not been idle. From a tinker he had heard
that Florence, Walter and the baby had been seen at the
York races. The sisters were hopping with excitement
when we told them our news. Madge seemed to recall
playing in a tin bath with a little girl who was having

trouble growing a full moustache, and that their mummy was very annoyed about it, and ground out her cigar in a footman's wig. Without more ado, the five of us set forth for Stratford.

The town was alive with merrymaking when our small contingent arrived. Food-stalls sold roast pig and fine ox tongues, chump chops and jams. The smell was enough to make one's mouth water. There was a fairground and dancing bears, flute and drum bands and dancers, gypsies telling fortunes and muscle-men wrestling in competition. Casks of ales and kegs of wine lay atop rough wooden tables, and intoxicated couples writhed on the ground nearby, fondling each other.

The townspeople threw curious glances at Quasimodo as we walked about. I heard shouts of, 'Get someone to put you up to it, Tiny' and 'Ask one of them for a date, they might put you on their short list'. How the little chap kept calm, I know not, but once or twice I saw his knuckles whiten as he gripped his sword-hilt. Not one of those louts knew how close to death they came.

It wasn't difficult to find Shakespeare's house. We asked one coarse local, who grinned horribly and muttered, 'Willy's the dog's bollocks.' When we knocked on the door, a voice rang out, telling the knocker to leave the rent for this week.

Undeterred, I knocked again, and this time the door opened, and there stood William Shakespeare himself. 'I'm just finishing off *Hamlet*,' he announced proudly.

At once, I apologized for interrupting his meal, and asked him to finish eating his egg.

He looked puzzled. 'What egg, pray?'

'The one you're eating.'

'I'm not eating an egg.'

'You are – an omelette.'

'I think your brains are scrambled.'

'Don't say that – I'm hard-boiled with insults.'

'Well, you should go back in your shell ... you're cracked.'

'I'll lose my top in three minutes.'

'This isn't my day ... come back later this week, say fried egg.'

Suddenly, the penny dropped, and we all started laughing at my silly mistake. Then Madge decided to come straight to the point and said that she suspected Shakespeare was really a woman, and possibly her sister.

William pursed his lips and cried, 'The time has come to show the world what I'm really like.' And with that he pulled off a plastic bald head and long curls shot out. He wriggled out of his clothes and stood before us in a whalebone corset and denim French knickers. 'Yes, it's true! I am a woman and you have freed me at last. Now is the winter of our discontent made glorious summer, etc., etc.'

'Can you remember what your mother's name was?' Beryl asked.

Wilhelmina thought for a moment, then her face lit up, but I threw a glass of water over her and quickly put the fire out. 'Yes, dear sisters. My mother's name was ... Florence.'

Another daughter had been found, and my head reeled with the discovery.

'I think that just about wraps it up,' said Madge. 'There can't be many more of us.' I was inclined to agree with her ... but how wrong I turned out to be.

Quasimodo and I needed a break, and decided to return to Paris for a few days. England was all right, but I missed the pavement cafés of the Left Bank, I yearned for the bustling life of the boulevards and I was sick of the smell of English horse-shit. (In France they sifted it daily.) The girls said they'd stay with their new-found sister until we came back, and would we please bring them some duty-free perfume, brandy and fags.

We set sail a few days later. It was a good deal from a package holiday firm, full-board and a cabin with private sanitary bucket. The crossing from Newhaven was awful. Violent rain lashed at us, and the ship pitched and tossed. In fact, it got so bad, seagulls started throwing us Kwells. The captain tried to avoid the storm by tacking and veering, but it didn't help. His navigation was a bit off too, as I noticed when we ran aground at Gibraltar. Finally, however, we docked at Le Havre and Quasimodo and I took a coach to Paris.

Life seemed to have quietened down in the metropolis (at least I didn't see any heads lying about), and when we reached the centre, we parted company. Quasimodo made for Notre-Dame, to see how they were coping, now that the bell-ringers' union had introduced a forty-hour week. As for me, I went to visit a mistress I had once dallied with ... she'd been a dilly to dally with, and when I saw her again we tore each other's clothes off and did some fruity things – and why not? She was a fair damson with a plum job, and I knew we made a handsome pear. Although I wasn't nuts about her, I didn't want her raisin her hopes, because she'd once told me that she wouldn't get married unless her sister Anna could live with her. Well, I'd met her sister and I knew that if my mistress and I got together, I'd have to ban Anna, because she hung around with a rotten bunch.

As I sat at a pavement table on the Rue D'Honoré one evening, I looked up from my coffee to see the familiar elegant figure of my old companion, Louis Bovary. On his arm was a comely maiden, whom he introduced as Madame Bovary, his great-aunt. It turned out that he'd gone into business with a Tunisian gentleman called Sheikh Rittel-Anrol, though everyone called him 'Rill'. They'd invented a food novelty together, Bovril, and it was going down a storm.

Louis seemed very happy, and blushingly confessed that he'd fallen in love with a girl who modelled for painters. 'She is so beautiful, Pierre,' he murmured. 'Come with me tomorrow to the Louvre, for in there does a portrait of my sweetheart hang.' (Lord, how I wished he could get his words in the right order!)

The following day, as arranged, we met outside the great museum with our tickets and a bag of mint imperials. Louis couldn't wait to show me the painting, and I must admit the enigmatic smile did make me think. Think, yes . . . the line of the jaw, the shape of the chin . . . Suddenly I knew with sickening certainty that I was looking at yet another of Florence's children.

I insisted that Louis took me to meet Mona Lisa at once. Eagerly, he agreed and we set off in the direction of Sèvres Babylon. At last, our coach and four drew up outside a modest residence in a somewhat shabby area. The front door opened, and there she stood – the Mona Lisa. After the introductions Louis offered her some Bovril, but she declined, saying, 'No thanks, chuck, but Mar Mite.'

After a pun like that, I looked at her, gravy like. 'Mona Lisa,' I said. 'I have reason to believe that you're not what you seem to be, or, to put it another way, nor are you what seems to be.'

Mona Lisa didn't turn a hair. 'Yes, you're right, Pierre. I know that what I am about to tell you will be a devastating shock, dear Louis, but I can no longer deceive you.' With that, she shrugged off her pretty frock, threw off the black wig and there before us was a short stocky man in his mid-forties, and he'd obviously bought his underpants from someone built much bigger down below . . . they weren't Y-fronts so much as W-fronts, back and centre.

His story was remarkable. He was the eldest son of

the redoubtable Florence, and born in Paris, the result of an affair between his mother and a man with bad eyesight. As far back as he could remember, Florence had dressed him as a girl, and of course he accepted this as the norm, although he got a lot of stick from his fellow tin-miners.

'I dimly recall a lot of children in the bed,' he said. 'If you went to the lavatory during the night, you had to use a bookmark to keep your place. I remember that Mother never employed a babysitter, it was always a shepherd. Oh, by the way, I was christened Ramona, but now I shall be known as Ramon. Thank you. At last I can stand up to take a leak.'

My poor heart-broken friend had sobbed helplessly while Ramon spoke, but I gave him a bun with jam in it and he soon bucked up.

Ramon travelled back to England with Quasimodo and me, and there was quite a reunion when the girls met their brother.

From time to time, wandering knights sent word that Florence and Walter had been spotted, but I suspected most of these were a case of over-zealous imagination. However, reliable Sir Lancelot reported that apparently Walter the Moron was fighting for the House of York against Lancaster. By all accounts, he had bounced a full division out of action at Naseby, and the Yorkshire side were paying him ten bob an hour with free bugle lessons thrown in.

Off we set, trekking across the Pennines to that mist-shrouded land called Yorkshire, home to a grim, dour race whose motto was 'If tha ever does owt fer nowt, do it fer thee sen', and who fed their sick-folk with Yorkshire Puddings on a drip.

Leeds had all the charm of a Senegal crematorium and Bradford was a sort of target area for starlings to shit on. Filey, on the other hand, was a seaside town, and usually shut. Occasionally something would happen, giving every Yorkshire heart a reason to rejoice, such as the Black Death, advanced cholera or a Lancashire man losing his loose change. However, as noted in that excellent book *How to Grow Dates in a Tuba* by A Machinist, Yorkshire only exists to keep the wind off Lancashire. They hung poor Dick Turnip because he refused to bank with the Halifax Building Society, which in those days was mainly thatched. It was a fierce conflict, the War of the Roses, and more soldiers were seen off by greenfly than bullets. Wherever we went it was the same story – the Lancashire lads would have won hands down, if it hadn't been for Walter.

A grisly rumour existed that if the Yorkists had a prisoner who refused to say where the pre-packed Lancashire hot-pot and cow-heel flans were hidden, they'd show him a sketch of Florence taking a shower. Within minutes, it was said, he'd tell all. Things were going badly for Lancashire and no mistake, and the Southport Flower Show was a complete wash-out that year.

It wasn't until the war was nearly over (due to failing light) that I finally spotted Walter, sat outside a catering cart and enjoying a plate of boiled horse and mashed potato. From time to time, a Lancastrian prisoner would be handed over, and he'd bounce the poor bugger up and down a hill.

When he was quite alone, I crept up from behind a bush and whispered, 'Hello, Walter. Do you remember me? Pierre Le Toq, your friend.'

Obviously, he hadn't a clue who I was, and he started bouncing me against a cannon. Thrice thus I went up and down, until he tired of this game and started to wind me round a cannon wheel.

'I like you, Mr Man,' Walter said as he stretched my neck, prior to using it as a catapult.

'I like you too, Walter,' I managed to croak as he spun me round by two fingers before drop-kicking me into a tub of spent cartridges.

Oddly enough, it was Quasimodo who saved me. 'Ding-dong, ding-dong,' he called out as Walter was tying my chest and thighs together in a reef knot.

'The bells, the bells! I know what they are saying,' the blithering idiot ranted at once, but he let me go and started jumping up and down, singing:

> 'The Captain of this lugger
> Was an ill-forsaken bugger.
> He wasn't fit
> To shovel shit
> From one ship to another.'

Eventually, by hitting Walter on the head with a sledge-hammer, Quasimodo got him to remember who we were and then the moron laughed and cried, 'You are my pals, Mr Men.'

Soon it was a happy domestic scene as we bathed him, and one could almost forgive what Walter was shaking in the water. Suffice it to say that I thought he'd found a model submarine at first . . . but enough of that.

All of a sudden the bathroom door fell off its hinges, and a five-foot three-inch baby in a romper suit and bowler hat strode in and started beating me up.

I managed to fight the infant off with a rusk, yelling, 'Quasimodo, this must be Florence's new baby . . . Look at the size of it . . . I can't have been the father. It must be Walter's.' I felt enormously happy and relieved, even though the babe was holding me in a Boston Crab. Luckily Florence walked in just as I began to black out. She picked up the baby, rammed his bottom into a brass chamber-pot and glared at me.

I took the bull by the horns. I wasn't going to let her cow me. It was cold in that bathroom. In fact, I was friesian. She scared me though, and I wished there were udders in the room. I had to stand on tiptoe to look her in the eyes, and my calves felt stiff and grazed.

'We know all about you, Florence,' I spluttered as she picked me up in one hand. 'And I have the rest of your family here with me.'

She dumped me in a jar with an onion in it and I knew I was in a pickle. Then, to my astonishment, she began to cry into a piece of sandpaper. 'My lovely daughters,' she wailed over and over again. 'Oh, I must see them, my own little loves.'

When they saw Florence, I sensed that her children felt an overwhelming impulse to run. But when she boomed out, 'I am your mummy', they rushed into her arms and snuggled close. It was a ghastly sight. After a while, Florence sat down and took the top off a bottle of beer with her teeth, while her children spread themselves at her feet.

Should I live to be a hundred and more, I doubt that I will ever hear a story to match the sizzling romance that had been Florence's life. Even today I find it hard to believe that I lived through such times. You, dear readers, are my jury. I have simply copied down the story that Florrie told that night . . .

READERS' JOKE COMPETITION

Why did the chicken cross the road knowing full well that some bugger would say it was perverted and make out that there was something peculiar about Thursday? . . . The reason the chicken crossed the road was because it was deaf . . . Ha, ha, ha.

(That interesting speculation was sent into the office wrapped around a coping stone. The name of the sender appears to be a certain Mr Eustace Cattermolesbury. His address is given as The Ninth Bunk, The Glass Eye Museum, Copper's Bottom, Iceland. We strongly suspect that Eustace is playing the fool, for we found out that during the Boer War he was not even born and it wasn't until his mother went to have a cyst lanced in 1925 that she realized she was pregnant. Eustace was born with a broken arm . . . he'd been hanging on until after the wedding. Eustace married a trumpet tuner in a haggis silo in the blackout and couldn't keep his knees straight in the pictures. His wife threw herself into a suitcase and got lost at Heathrow. Eustace never got over the loss of the suitcase. Always a joker. Eustace made a video of his legs whispering in a conduit shed.)

WHEN THE BOOK ENDS, DON'T FORGET THE POSTSCRIPT AND READERS' COMMENTS . . .

FLORENCE

Her story started long ago and far away, in a village that clung to the side of a Himalayan mountain.

One day there was great excitement in the village. The corpse of a yeti had been found in a hole half-way up Mount Everest by a sherpa who had come to sell yak milk to the local primary school. The vast hairy monster was dragged into the village square, and the mayor said, 'Farfed n'a Pli to bumm', which freely translated means, 'We should cop a few quid now, lads.'

At once a quick-witted councillor wrote to a man he knew who knew a woman who was engaged to a man whose son was friends with a set of twins who knew a bareback circus rider. The letter reported the discovery of the Abominable Snowman, and asked if someone from Chipperfield's circus could send a lot of money and something to put the yeti in before it went off, so to speak.

The note was attached to a pigeon's foot, and off it flew. Unfortunately, the note was written on slate, and the pigeon plummeted into a crevasse, where it froze as it was laying an egg.

What the simple villagers didn't know, however, was that the dead yeti was a female . . . it had died waiting for the end of this book. And its mate was already approaching the village, looking for his missis. All unknowing, the villagers covered the dead yeti in ice, stuck a sell-by date on it and shoved it under a supermarket.

Meanwhile, a young Tibetan maiden was on her way to the village to marry the headman's son. As she trotted across the mountain ridge on a rent-a-mule from Llasa, she failed to notice the twelve-foot yeti behind her. She saw the danger too late . . . the monster plucked her from the mule's back, which it then bent into the shape of a duck, and carried her off to a nearby snow motel.

The maiden never mentioned her encounter with the yeti, but people were always commenting on her wide smile. The wedding went ahead as planned. The catering was supplied by a Cash and Curry firm and priced most reasonably at £10 a head . . . and they were big heads. There was dancing and horseplay and everybody got drunk. A comedian from Nepal told a joke about a man buying a hen, thinking it was a cockerel, and his wife said, 'Well, in that case, him a layer!' And a heckler shouted, 'Don't you Everest?' which went down so well they paid the comic off.

Nine months later the maiden gave birth to a baby. The midwife took one look and threw herself off a cliff. The doctor lost his memory and started charging his patients the right money, and the maiden's husband went home to his mother in Carlisle.

Enraged by the way she had been treated, the new mother took her child and vanished into the night. The wilderness would be their home from now on.

Although the baby, a girl, was horrible to look at, the young woman fed her wisely – on wild elk meat and eagle *garni* and, as the years passed, the she-child prospered, growing into a normal nine-foot girl.

The child was named 'Child of a Thousand Winds Blowing from the Mountains of Yamah the Great God

of the Far Snows that Lie Beyond the No-bottom Waters
of the Eternal Lake', but 'Florence' was written on the
birth certificate.

It was a harsh life, and eventually, when Florence
was fourteen, mother and daughter made their way to a
town. Florence managed to get a job working as a
bouncer in a yak-hide tannery and tearooms, where she
kept the rough mountain hunters in line by threatening
to sleep with them. Her mother opened a billiard hall
and started going out with a monk who'd got fed up
staying indoors. It was this monk who took Flo's mum
back to the wilderness and fixed her up with the yeti
who'd made her so happy that first wonderful time.

The monk persuaded Florence to stay in the town, and
to try slipping a bag over her head whenever she went to
the shops. Before long, Flo had a large collection of
differently styled bags.

One day in the tearooms, Florence was introduced to a
French butterfly collector who had been forced to move
from his home next to a nudist colony because of his
failing eyesight. Florence didn't realize how bad the
Frenchman's sight was until she saw him pick up a
snake to kill a stick.

The first time the poor fool asked her to sleep with
him, she readily agreed . . . and her life would never be
the same again. He took her back to France to help him
choose a pair of bi-focals so that he could 'see the beauty'
of his bride. But Florence painted over the lenses of the
new spectacles. 'My eyes are getting worse, *ma chérie*,'
her husband moaned. 'I must buy stronger glasses.'

Every time he bought a new pair of specs, Flo painted
them, and eventually he gave up and made love to her
by Braille. In quick succession, Florence gave birth to
seven children – five girls and two boys. Then one night,
her short-sighted lover took Florence to the opera, and
soon people were screaming and jumping off the
balcony.

It was all too much for the young woman. Over the years, her mother's bitter hatred against men had seeped into her own heart, and now she wanted her revenge. That same evening, Florence hung a sign saying 'Help' in Braille round her myopic husband's neck and pushed him into the Seine.

At once, she put her plans into action. Telling her children that it was a man's world, she dressed the girls in boys' clothing and forced her sons into girls' clothes to humiliate them. Then they were sent away to find their destinies, and reminded not to forget to send some housekeeping money home.

And so Florence became a whore, lurking in dark places. And as she practised her art in that darkness, she learned many secrets, and so grew dangerous and powerful throughout Paris.

Ah, yes, dear reader, that night Florrie told us of how, despite herself, she had fallen for Walter the Moron, and of how they had made love one night at a wine auction behind a Saxon brick kiln . . . and, indeed, she glowed with happiness.

Proudly, her children told her their own stories, and when she saw how well they had done for themselves, her contentment knew no bounds. Her only sadness was in learning that Ethel – famous throughout Europe as Horatio Nelson – was now alas as dead as mutton, and she cried silently for a couple of minutes, using up three sheets of sandpaper.

When she had recovered, Florence congratulated Madge on her success as Henry the Eighth, and, rather less enthusiastically, Irene on her life as Guy Fawkes. As for Wilhelmina, Florence was full of admiration. The girl's plays were popular hits, and she'd just opened her third deposit account with Nationwide. Beryl was a tricky one. After all, apart from a few newspaper articles and the odd battle, Beryl as Bonnie Prince

Charlie hadn't really made it big. And as for the hair
dye she'd used, well, it looked completely wrong with her
fair complexion.

It soon became apparent to all of us that Flo couldn't
make up her mind about Ramon either. All he'd done
was pose for a painting – and he still hadn't been paid
for it. 'All right,' Flo allowed, 'I agree, Da Vinci's a good
painter. He can do a living room in primer and two coats
of gloss in under an hour, but immortality . . . ?'

'Excuse me, Florence,' I said softly, 'what happened to
your other son?' But the poor woman had no idea. All
she remembered was giving him a bugle and a chocolate
biscuit.

Then our words died on our lips, for at that moment
we were all arrested as Bonnie Prince Charlie's spies.
The alarm had been given by an alert Quaker who knew
his oats, and didn't wheat a second to tell the authorities
about us. People used to chaff at this Quaker because he
had a big corn on his foot and had to keep buying
bran-new shoes. Anyway, this story isn't a cereal, so I'll
carry on before I get lost in a maize of words.

A patrol of the Queen's Dragoons escorted us to
London to stand trial. Oddly enough, neither Quasimodo
nor Walter offered any resistance. In fact, weariness
seemed to have swept over them . . . just as though
they'd been reading this book . . .

We weren't locked up in the Tower for long, because it
had already been booked by a Japanese industrialist for
his son's barmitzvah. More to the point, Queen
Elizabeth wanted an early trial.

The courtroom was packed on that first day, and, oh,
how the people sniggered at the evidence given that
Madge, Beryl, Irene and Wilhelmina had in fact been
Henry the Eighth, Bonnie Prince Charlie, Guy Fawkes
and William Shakespeare. The suggestion that Ramon
was also the Mona Lisa drew the biggest laugh of all,

but when Quasimodo claimed to be the Blade of
Passion, the judge had hysterics and asked us whether
we'd ever been on *Opportunity Knocks*. The press
labelled us the 'Crazy Gang', and we were offered a split
week's booking at the Victoria Palace.

The trial was number one in the ratings. You couldn't
get into the courtroom unless you had an Equity card.
Finally, our stupid lawyer decided to play his trump
card and tell the court that the late Lord Nelson was
really Ethel. Of course I tried to stop him, and I set down
here the action-packed drama which ensued:

JUDGE: 'Silence, Le Toq, or I'll hold you in
contempt.'
ME: 'You can't because I don't recognize this court.'
JUDGE: 'Why not?'
ME: 'Because you've had it decorated.'
JUDGE: 'Is this the first time you've been up before
me?'
ME: 'I don't know, what time do you normally get up?'

The crowded courtroom gasped at this bitter tirade
and a man went round selling hot puddings on a stick.
After the statement that Lord Nelson had been a
woman called Ethel, the atmosphere in the courtroom
changed. Gone was the mood of bonhomie; in its place
lurked grim loathing. How dare we say such a terrible
thing? This time the joke had gone too far, and now they
wanted our blood. The judge sentenced each and every
one of us to be executed. Our fate was sealed.

Time in the Tower sped by and death was our
constant companion. In the small square outside they
were building a bigger stage for the block, because the
demand for tickets had exceeded everyone's expecta-
tions. The people whose houses overlooked the site were
renting out window space for the big day.

Then we heard that Queen Elizabeth the First herself was going to attend the executions. It seemed she had followed the case with interest and wanted to see us die for our infamy. Our hearts sank, and Florence bequeathed her teeth to science. But they said they'd contest the will.

To pass the time away we played five-a-side chess and sang songs. Walter bounced mice in a corner and Florence did press-ups. Finally, on a damp Tuesday morning, we were told that our appeal for clemency had been turned down, because they couldn't find Clements.

All too soon it was time for our last breakfast . . . our last meal on this earth . . . but why Moon over it? We didn't planet this way, did we? How I wished I was with my family, back at Mars, Saturn her sofa, hearing her shout, 'Get up them stars' . . . I had been her favourite Sun and now I had come to this . . .

The jailers said we could order what we liked, and so Florence chose plover's eggs with a mixed grill, toast and a leg of pork and minced truffles in lettuce sauce. Walter went for a full baked cow with Patna rice and aubergines, followed by a pig's head stuffed with diced apple and coleslaw. Bery, Irene and Wilhelmina all opted for cornflakes, low-fat beans on brown bread and various kinds of seafood pâté with Weightwatcher's apple strudel to finish, and Madge's selection was a simple meal of marinated sea-lion with chips and marrowfat peas, hot cheeses filled with oyster skins in batter, and a large plate of spotted dick. I seemed to have lost my appetite altogether. Quasimodo had a banana, ate it quickly, climbed inside the skin and Florence sewed him in. At least one of us had a chance.

As we pushed our empty plates away we heard the muttered incantation of priests and the heavy footsteps of the guards. They had come to take us to the place of death . . . just a short walk around the block. It was a chance to get a head if you had a large sharp blade, but I decided not to axe. Soon I knew they'd axe me to stick my neck out, but with the recession, I'd soon be for the chop.

Bright sunshine blinded us as we left the gloomy Tower and stepped out on to the platform. Before us were eight wooden blocks. In the square below, vendors were selling hot dogs and pies from a mock-up of the Savoy Grill. There was a huge crowd of people, all waiting to see us die. One smart-arsed official noticed that there were only seven of us, so Quasimodo's ruse was discovered. 'Is the little git a fruit?' someone shouted, and the mob roared in approval. Personally, I thought the remark showed extremely poor taste.

Suddenly, massed trumpets heralded the arrival of Her Majesty, Queen Elizabeth the First of England. She waved regally to the crowd, and a lady-in-waiting handed her a programme. Meanwhile the executioner was honing his blade and the sparks brought some colour to an otherwise bleak scene. The drum roll sounded, the death sentence was read out and the crowd gasped at Florence's mighty head. Beneath Quasimodo's block sat a bowl of custard . . . it raised a laugh, but not as big as the writers had expected. (He was still in his banana skin, you see? No? Oh, never mind!)

Then a hush spread through the crowd . . . all eyes were on Florence.

'The first to be put to death in this, the main event, will be the celebrated Whore of Paris, Florence. Have you any last words before we make you a lot shorter?'

Calmly Florence spat in the man's face. Then she said in a loud clear voice, effectively drowning out the noise of an all-steel slave band, 'Get stuffed, you pathetic crud.'

At that moment I happened to glance across at Queen Elizabeth. Her face had drained of blood, her mouth was agape. Slowly she rose to her feet, her finger trembling as she pointed towards the scene of execution. 'STOP!' she screamed out loud as the axe began to fall.

The silence was intent, but noisy outside the tent. As the crowd stared, the Queen jumped from the stand and ran towards the platform, where she embraced Florence, shouting with great joy as she did so. 'Mummy, mummy! It's your little boy! It's me, Mummikins – your son Bernard Harry!'

It caused a sensation, and the price of pies went up two pence. Quickly Bernard pulled off his red wig, the crown, ruff and the jewelled frock and stood there in his football shorts and vest. Florence reached out and kissed him, weeping. You would have wept too, dear, sensitive reader, because Bernard was wearing Everton colours.

We were set free of course, and at last Florence was reunited with the rest of her family. She and Walter were married before Broadmoor could lay claim to him. It was a moving ceremony . . . it was held on the tail-board of a van. Louis Bovary came over from France for the reception at a newly thatched Holiday Inn, and as the evening progressed, he and Beryl began flirting outrageously. Quasimodo turned down an offer to stay in England as Bernard's bodyguard, and accepted a job as head bell-ringer at Notre-Dame. And why not? He knew the ropes, and had a lot of pull. What's more, he was fast, he could go like the clappers. So I didn't think he was dropping a clanger. As for myself, I saw that Wilhelmina was looking most favourably in my direction, and suddenly I felt that familiar tingle up my leg . . . my bike-clips were scratching.

Well, my friends, that is the real story of history. All the things you were told in school were just pathetic attempts to hide the truth. They were tempestuous times. Times of great feats . . . and legs too, of course. If I didn't mention them it would be toe bad, and one must keep instep these days. Some men I knew were fine and others were heels, some men led a pure life, others shinned. But time has passed, and many many years have gone by since I first penned this stirring epic. Wilhelmina and I live over a tobacconist's in Stratford now, and it can be a real drag climbing those stairs . . . at least, I find it a fag. S'nuff of these dreadful puns, though. I'm getting on in years now, although I've never filtered better, and I'm at least ten pounds lighter. As for my memory, it's unimpaired. Go on, ash me anything you like. The only thing is, I get tired easily . . . in fact, I'm shagged now.

Wilhelmina's doing very well. Her new play, *A Midsummer Night's Dream*, is currently showing at the Globe, and the whole production is staged on Walter's stomach. He and Florence have since had five more children. Sadly, I haven't heard from Quasimodo or his bells, but there again, I suppose it's a sign of the chimes. Robin and Marian? Well, he's selling timber in Nottingham. Marian said that if he wants to do that it's oak by her, and that's plane enough. She would have liked to live near a beech, but that wouldn't be fir on Robin. Always a nice dresser, Robin is still spruce, and likes to cross his palms with silver. But with all the money he's got, you'd think he'd be sycamore. At any rate, he's lumbered with firewood, and there's a new timbre in his voice. He keeps a log book and is planning to open another branch soon, but Marian's twigged that, and she's not one to beat about the bush.

Beryl and Ramon are coming over tomorrow night for a fish supper, because our local chippy is the best plaice for it. In the words of the song: 'Nobody know the turbots I've seen' or, alternatively, am I my brother's kipper?

*

Despite Wilhelmina's success, she's not getting paid as much as she should, and men like Marlowe and Bacon are claiming to have written her plays. Marlowe even went as far as to say that he had written *Macbeth* as a comedy and sent it to Shakespeare, who was acting as his literary agent in Birmingham.

Mayhap this book will propel me into the halls of immortality, but that, dear reader, must be left up to you.

> Pierre Le Toq
> Flat 1a
> Hagboiled Alley
> Stratford
> S75 5DR

FINI

POSTSCRIPT

There have been so many near riots outside bookshops in protest about what marginally intelligent people have called, 'The biggest load of infantile bullshit ever perpetrated on the British public by a so-called writer' that the whole point of Mr Dawson's novel has been lost in the furore.

Some years ago I was, and still am, basically convinced that Lloyd George is in fact Martha Entwhistle from Bagshot. The way he walked and used his hands took me back to the days when I was a water-diviner with Selfridges and courted a girl from Baghdad who spoke perfect Welsh and lived in a basement flat with a bassoon moulder. She was the spitting image of Lloyd George.

I have since tried to find Martha Entwhistle many times, but at every point I have come up against a brick wall, which makes me think she might well have been a hod carrier.

I go to the library most days, looking through back-issues in case I uncover anything about Martha, or Lloyd George for that matter, but she has completely disappeared. I did hear from an old lady who reckoned she dated Lloyd George once, and when she took his long john's off for a parliamentary frolic, she couldn't feel any testicles. But it was late November when she had this encounter, so if it was very cold and she had forgotten to warm her hands, his equipment might well have retracted into a memory.

I found the book fascinating and the author's grasp of history quite astounding. Please accept a cheque for five pounds to help Mr Dawson to get back into the country.

Must dash, they are very strict about meal-times in here and they think I'm Mother Goose.

Meredith Puddle
Ward 8
Home for the Chronically Cracked
Fasnet

READERS' LETTERS

Dear Sirs,

My great-great-grandmother, who left a foundry to a Mormon charity, once wrote to a close friend that after shaking hands with Queen Victoria she had been astounded by the strength of the monarch's grip, and the heavy muscular development of her upper arms.

Later on, at a chamber-music recital at Osborne House, conducted by Signor Jerri from the Po valley, a lady-in-waiting just happened to mention that she had only that day returned from Italy, from the city of Florence, in fact.

What stunned the glittering assembly was that, upon hearing the word 'Florence', Queen Victoria stood up shakily and whispered, 'Mummy'.

Having ploughed through Mr Dawson's drivel, I must say that although the book is a load of crap, the story told by my grandmother does somehow leave a doubt in one's mind, and on that basis, I do feel that we should try to secure Mr Dawson's release.

In anticipation,
Miss Dottie Kangaroo

Dere Surr,

I thort the book was gud, butt ther was a lot off big wurds witch I did'ent understannd. My daddy threw'd the book on the fire, but I got if off with a poker and read it. Is Mr Dawson as barmi as they say?

Roderick Pump, aged 37

My dear publishers,

I have in my time read books written by imbeciles and idiots, but for progressive asininity, this garbage was beyond recall.

Yours faithfully,
Chief Running Moon
Forest Reservation
Montana
USA

17th-CENTURY JOKES

I'm not saying that thy house is small . . . but
thy mice have to walk about on their hands.

I'm not saying that thy house is damp . . . but
thou daren't go into the cellar unless thou art
wearing shark repellent.

I'm not saying that thy ship is old . . . but
they started it with a whip.

I'm not saying that thy wife is fat . . . but
her skin has stretched to such an extent, when she
bends her knees her eyelids fly open.

I'm not saying, madam, that thy husband is thin . . . but
every time he swallows tomato juice, builders use him as
a spirit level.

I'm not saying that thy wife is ugly . . . but
she went for a swim in Loch Ness and the monster got
out and picketed the lake.

I'm not saying that my wife is a fast eater . . . but
when she sits at the dining-room table, her elbows are in
starting blocks.

I'm not saying my wife is ignorant . . . but
when she asked the butcher where he got his meat from
and he answered, 'Bullocks', she said, 'I thought it was
neck end.'

I would not say that we are posh . . . but
we get pickled cabbage through Interflora.